VAMPIRES and Cream

ZENOBIA RENQUIST

DZRB BOOKS

FOREWORD

Student loan debt and a lustful vampire are the least of her worries.

To pay off the expensive training Jeliyah received while becoming the strongest necromancer in her precinct, she has to team up with a centuries' old vampire who dresses gangsta and loves the thrill of the kill. Hunting rogue vampires is the purpose of their partnership, but Teaghan seems more interested in getting Jeliyah into bed.

Both their priorities change when a lucrative hunt goes wrong and lands them on the rogue list. For their continued survival, Jeliyah must use forbidden magic that binds them together, strengthening her but also awakening desires she wants to deny. Running for her life is not the time to indulge in pleasure, but not indulging and giving in fully could be the thing that gets her killed.

Note: This title was previously published under the title CREAM.

CHAPTER
ONE

High scores on all tests, deadeye status in marksmanship, and commendations in spell casting—Jeliyah was palladium level, which was the highest level in the necromancer middle class, only about half a step away from upper class. She had earned her standing long ago, and the day had finally come for her to get an enforcer.

Enforcer. That was what the humans called them. The vampires called them bounty hunters and worse. They were opportunistic vampires who hunted rogues for the thrill of the kill and the rewards. Human government types had preferred a less provocative title when the human-vampire cooperation started. Bounty hunters became enforcers. A little whitewash to make everyone feel warm and cozy.

It didn't matter what they were called. That didn't change the job or how they did it. Enforcers partnered with human vampire hunters, also known as necromancers, to kill rogues and were paid a hefty sum for every rogue eliminated. If Jeliyah had been stationed anywhere else, she would have been partnered with an enforcer the moment she arrived for her assignment after graduation.

She glared at the back of Hirsch's head. Her boss had been making her ride a desk since she was assigned to his division three years ago. He'd used every excuse he could pull out of his ass to keep her at that desk—not enough hunts to go around, no available enforcers, the enforcers preferred not to work with women, and other crap that reeked worse than his cheap knockoff cologne. It all boiled down to him not wanting her there.

Hirsch's division had been all men until the trustees slapped him with an equal-opportunity citation and then shoved Jeliyah his way. She didn't appreciate being the token in this situation. The trustees had interfered again when they noticed Jeliyah being passed over for enforcer assignments continuously for the third year in a row, which looked highly suspicious because the new guys—who were rose gold level at the highest, thus they were far below Jeliyah—were being partnered with an enforcer two seconds after stepping foot in the building.

"And here she is," Hirsch said as he swung the door wide and entered the room where the enforcer waited.

Jeliyah's necrome amulet—a flat, coin-sized disc with an intricate dragon etched onto one side and a tiger on the other— hummed softly against her collarbone, alerting her to the presence of the vampire. She didn't need the warning, but was glad it worked the way it should.

The vampire stood with his hip resting against the back of the couch and one hand in the pocket of his suit slacks. The shades over his eyes completed Jeliyah's idea of how an enforcer should appear—menacing and mysterious. Anyone else wearing shades indoors would be obnoxious, but vampires abhorred fluorescent light. They said it was too harsh and left an afterimage, like staring at the sun.

Jeliyah tried to keep calm and maintain a steady heart rate so the vampire wouldn't realize how excited she was. A partner at last. Ever since being identified as palladium level, Jeliyah had looked forward to working with an enforcer. Years of training would finally have a purpose.

After placing her duffel bag near the door, she walked forward and held out her hand. "I'm Jeliyah Parsons." She smiled when the vampire shook her hand. "I look forward to working with you."

The man grinned, showing his long canines. "That's sweet, but I'm not your partner. I'm Fredrick, the messenger." He jerked his thumb over his shoulder. "He's your partner."

Jeliyah looked in the direction he indicated, not happy she hadn't realized there were two vampires in the room. That was dangerous and sloppy and not completely her fault since the man had been sitting in a high-backed chair that obscured him from sight. Still, excuses like that were the reason necromancers died in this line of work rather than retiring.

She moved forward as the chair swiveled around. "Nice to meet you. I'm—" Her greeting and her smile died on her lips.

The man sitting on the chair pulled his shades down with one finger hooked around the edge and moved his ice-blue gaze over Jeliyah. He nodded as he edged his shades back in place and stood up. With his fist held out to the other vampire, he said, "Good looking out."

The suited vampire bumped fists with the man while Jeliyah tried to come to terms with her new partner. He wasn't at all what she had imagined after reading his file. Teaghan was a top enforcer with hundreds of kills under his belt, a fifth of those after the human-vampire cooperative started.

He'd retired seven partners in the last three years, which was high by anyone's standards. Most partnerships lasted a minimum of one year before a necromancer was close to retirement. With Teaghan's kill rate, a necromancer only needed to stay by his side for a few months.

Someone with a record like that should be the stoic, no-nonsense type. Jeliyah had been prepared for the militant type with a chip on his shoulder because he had to babysit a human, even if that human was giving him the edge he needed to keep his kill count so high.

Instead, what she got flaming-red hair in neat cornrows that ended past his shoulders, a tight black tank top with thick gold chains draped over it, baggy jeans that were two sizes too big, and tan work boots with the laces untied. His only saving grace was that he knew how to use a belt, though that didn't change the fact that a vampire born in the seventeen hundreds was dressed gangsta.

This had to be a joke. Jeliyah looked at Hirsch. He was all smiles. The happy smiles of a man getting what he wanted, not the joking smiles people wore right before telling someone they'd been punked.

Teaghan sucked his teeth, and Jeliyah glanced at him in time to see one of his elongated canines capped in gold. That was her limit. There were certain things she had been prepared to handle and others she had been prepared to ignore. She refused to consider him.

She pointed at Teaghan and asked in a low, hard tone, "What is that?"

Hirsch startled. "What did you say?" His happy smile turned placating as he faced the vampires. "Sorry for her attitude. Jeliyah is new to the field."

Teaghan stood. "S'all good, son."

"Oh, hell no." Jeliyah turned on her heel, grabbed her duffel bag and walked out of the room. No. Nope. Not happening. There weren't enough negative sentiments in the world to convey how much she would not work with *that*. Not when he looked and acted like the way he was.

She made it to the elevator before Hirsch grabbed her elbow. "Hold it, Parsons."

"Get off me." She glared at his hand until he released her and then turned the expression on him. Hirsch was her boss, but he was only silver level, which made him far weaker than her, and they both knew it. If it came to a fight, he would lose without Jeliyah having to do much.

"Where are you going?"

"Away from here. You are not sticking me with *that*."

Hirsch glanced over his shoulder as he made a loud shushing noise. He said between his teeth, "Lower your voice."

"Why?" Jeliyah stayed loud on purpose. "They're vampires, Hirsch. They could hear whatever I'm saying even if I was talking on the elevator."

The chime indicating the elevator had arrived sounded. Jeliyah looked between the four sets of doors to see which would open first.

Hirsch said, "Walk out now and you might as well pack your stuff."

"You can't fire me. This isn't that type of job."

"No, I can't fire you, but I can send your ass back where you came from."

She turned toward him. "What?"

He crossed his arms with a smug expression. "Go with Teaghan, or go back to the campus. Either way, you're out of my hair. I couldn't give a damn which one you pick, but know that you'll be going back to the campus with a rip."

"What rip?"

"Refusal of a direct order."

"You... You..." She gritted her teeth and clenched her fists. Hirsch knew she couldn't go back to the campus with something like that on her record. Necromancers were rare, so this wasn't a job from which they could fire her, but that didn't mean they couldn't punish her. An icy chill ran down her spine. "He can't be the only enforcer who needs a partner."

Hirsch grinned. "He's not. There were a few others, but I knew he would be the perfect fit for *you*."

Jeliyah bit back her first comment, the one where she told him to go fuck himself. She didn't like the man, and he sure as hell didn't like her, this being proof. But he could still give her a rip for insubordination if she said what she wanted.

"Up to you." He stepped back so she could see the doorway leading to the vampires and a future she wanted to deny.

"I'm filing a complaint," she said as she walked back to the room.

"On what grounds?"

"Racial harassment."

Hirsch shrugged his indifference. "It's not my fault he's like that. I merely matched a palladium level with a high-ranking enforcer like I'm supposed to. All the others rank beneath him. I wouldn't want the trustees thinking I wasn't using your full potential, now would I?"

She clamped her mouth shut against the litany of curses that begged to be given freedom. The sooner she got away from Hirsch, the better for her continued safety. That meant leaving with Teaghan, who stood watching the door with the other vampire.

Teaghan had the nerve to grin at her when she walked through the door. "Welcome back."

Her teeth scraped against each other as she held back more words she shouldn't say. Not yet. Not so long as Hirsch was there. As soon as she and Teaghan were alone, she planned to tell him just what she thought of him and his attitude.

"Let's go," she bit out.

Teaghan bumped fists with the other vampire again. "Thanks for dragging my sorry ass out here."

"Any time. Have fun."

"Plan to."

Jeliyah exhaled a frustrated breath and stalked away.

Hirsch called after her, "Good luck on your hunts, Jeliyah."

"Fuck you," she said under her breath. "Fuck you hard with a rusted, spiked dildo, you son of a diseased bitch."

Both vampires laughed. Jeliyah ignored them. She'd known they would hear her. Her concern was that Hirsch not hear her.

Rather than return to the elevators, she shoved open the door to the stairwell. Fifteen flights of stairs would work off some of her anger... she hoped. The situation might not be as bad as she thought. She was taking it at face value.

Teaghan was a top-ranked enforcer. No matter how he dressed or acted, he got the job done. If his track record held, she would only have to put up with his nonsense for the next four-to-six months. With the rogue incursions so high of late, their time together might be less than that. She hoped that was the case.

Endure. All she had to do was to endure. Not everyone got a dream assignment. Not everyone got an assignment. Retirement was around the corner. That would be her mantra until this nightmare ended.

She exited the necromancer headquarters and breathed in the early evening air. A cool, crisp autumn breeze soothed her heated skin.

"Feel better?" Teaghan asked, placing himself in the path of the breeze.

Jeliyah had to look up to meet his gaze, since the top of her head was level with his shoulder. She would like to say she had forgotten he was there. The hum of her necrome against her collarbone wouldn't let her forget.

"Fine," she snapped. A quick glance around showed no vehicles in the vicinity. She didn't have a car—couldn't afford one yet—so that meant riding with Teaghan. Joy.

Teaghan jerked his thumb to the company parking lot. "My ride's that way."

She prayed for something normal. She got a black convertible sports car—top down—that sat two people and had blue lightning racing along the sides. "Subtle."

"Fast." He hopped over the side and settled onto the seat. "You were expecting a lowrider, right?"

"Whatever." She opened the passenger door and dropped onto the seat with her duffel bag wedged between her legs. Emphasis on the drop. She hated sports cars for this reason. Any car that required putting her hand on the ground to get out of it was too low. Cars like that might be fast, but they were also death traps in a collision.

Of course, a vampire wouldn't worry about something like that. So long as his head and heart were intact, he could heal anything else.

"You can stash the bag in the trunk."

Yeah, that would make sense, though it surprised her the car had a trunk. But she was already seated. "Just drive."

"Whatever." Teaghan revved the engine to life and spun the tires before peeling out of the parking lot with the back end fishtailing.

Jeliyah sighed, not impressed. Cars didn't do it for her. She didn't know any woman who got off on cars and the tricks men did in them. Then again, most of her former female friends were necromancers as well. With their backgrounds, a man needed to be a platinum level before Jeliyah and her friends thought of him as potential dating material. Not that she had any delusions of catching the eye of a platinum level. A palladium level like herself, maybe. Possibly a gold level, but she would only settle for rose gold level at the lowest.

A platinum level was out of her reach, even if she managed to retire. Actually, everyone was out of her reach, retired or not. But retirement was still the goal. That was the only reason to put up with Teaghan.

The glint of a streetlamp off one of his gold chains made her sigh. If she could put up with him. Guys like him got on her nerves —misappropriating assholes.

Teaghan had been ready to put a bullet through Fredrick's skull when the man dragged him off a hunt to meet his new necromancer partner. After an entire month sitting on his ass, Teaghan had finally gotten a call for a hunt. Fredrick had decided that was as good a time as any to stick Teaghan with a partner who Teaghan had to meet right that moment.

There were two things Teaghan didn't tolerate—people interfering with his hunts, and people interfering with his money. Since his hunts made him money, Fredrick was on Teaghan's shit list... or he had been until Teaghan saw Jeliyah.

Actually, Fredrick had received a stay of execution the moment Teaghan caught Jeliyah's scent when she walked in the room. He'd drawn in a deep breath, inhaling her fragrance—cucumber and aloe mixed with cocoa butter. The cucumber-and-aloe scent came from her brown skin. That meant it was her body wash or lotion. The aroma of cocoa butter originated from her shoulder-length corkscrew afro black hair—hair grease was his first guess. The hint of something chemical under it all—also originating from her head —let him know she used gels to keep the curls defined.

All three distinct smells had revealed Jeliyah was Black and female before Teaghan had swiveled his chair around. She might be disappointed with him, but he found no fault with the way her jeans hugged her round hips and thick thighs, or how her ample breasts strained the buttons of her shirt. Add full lips begging to be kissed and brown eyes that flashed with anger the same way he knew they would shine with passion and Teaghan had a recipe for a woman he wouldn't mind being around for the next few months.

But he didn't like necromancers. If not for the vampire-human cooperative, he wouldn't have to put up with them. He did his job better than most without a necromancer at his side. The necromancers made him better, but they improved his competition, too. It was hard to enjoy the hunt and eventual kill when he had to worry about some asshole taking out the target before him.

"You been on a hunt before, sweetness?"

"My name is Jeliyah, not sweetness. And no, I haven't."

Teaghan rolled his eyes. Great. An amateur. That's just what he didn't need. "You're about to get a crash course. I got pulled off a hunt to meet you."

"Sorry to put you out," she said in a sarcastic tone.

"You're going to make it up to me, or I'm taking your ass right back."

Jeliyah inhaled softly and her heart rate sped up, letting Teaghan know he'd hit a nerve. He hadn't missed her earlier conversation with Hirsch about sending her back to the campus. Teaghan might not know what the big deal was about going back to the campus, but he knew necromancers who refused to do their job caught shit the likes of which he wouldn't wish on his worst enemy. Humans called vampires monsters, but vampires couldn't compete with cruelty like that.

He said, "Tell me you at least know what you're doing?"

"I'm palladium level."

"So?"

"Yes, I know what I'm doing," she snapped.

"Good." Teaghan grinned in the dark at her attitude, which further hinted at the presence of a backbone. At least she wasn't mousy. The last necromancer he'd been stuck with had spent the entire partnership cowering in the background, afraid Teaghan would turn on him. Teaghan had had to monitor his necromancer during hunts to make sure the man wouldn't attack Teaghan and the rogue at the same time.

After Teaghan retired that necromancer, he'd told the reserve to go fuck themselves—in as polite a manner as possible—when they requested he come in to get his next necromancer. The stupid vampire-human cooperative required all enforcers to have a necromancer at their sides during hunts. Teaghan refused. He didn't like babysitting humans. Hence why Fredrick had interfered with Teaghan's hunt. A hunt he'd had to almost beat out of the dispatcher since the man had refused to give Teaghan any hunts while he didn't have a partner.

If all Teaghan's future necromancers resembled Jeliyah, he'd be there to meet them two seconds after the current one announced retirement status. But he knew better. Teaghan was in Hirsch's jurisdiction, which meant all Teaghan's future necromancers would be men. He had to wonder who Jeliyah had pissed off to get stuck with Hirsch—or maybe it was the other way around. Small talk like that would have to wait for later, though.

He parked his car in the empty lot outside the forest that led to the Marceaux estate. Rogues had a bad habit of being predictable. Most were assassins sent by one of the European families to take out the head of a clan. America had fifteen vampire families who had divided the United States into territories. There were another ten families in Canada and two more controlled Mexico down through Panama. Those twenty-seven families formed a parliamentary system that ruled over the North American vampires. The only way for someone new to stake a claim—and become part of the parliament in one of the few nations that didn't kill vampires on sight—was to take out the family in charge of the location they wanted.

Power struggles like this were as old as the vampires themselves. Humans had gotten involved once vampires were outed during a nasty little skirmish in the fifties. Two warring families had gotten carried away and revealed the existence of vampires to the world. Fast-forward a few decades and Teaghan was stuck escorting a necromancer on a hunt to appease some live-and-let-live treaty the vampire parliament had signed to end vampire-hunting season... in North America, at least.

"Let's do this." He jumped out of the car then faced the necromancer.

She sucked in a deep breath before blowing it out and opening her car door. There was a brief struggle while she clambered over the duffel bag between her legs to get out. Teaghan didn't see this as a good start. Every vampire on the property could probably hear the noise she was making. That was another reason he didn't like necromancers. He might as well be hunting with a marching band following behind him. Humans didn't know how to be quiet, not quiet enough so vampire ears couldn't hear them.

Jeliyah opened her duffel bag and pulled out a gun shoulder harness and a palm-sized pouch. She put on the harness, then opened the pouch. Teaghan felt the power the second she opened it. This was the other reason he hated necromancers. Their weapons made his skin crawl. Him and every other vampire on the planet.

Necromancers wielded weapons made of metal and magic using a recipe passed down from vampire hunters of old. Not every human had been oblivious to vampires prior to the outing. A few had turned killing vampires—assassins hadn't always been rogues —into a lucrative business. The most famous of which were the Van Helsings, who humans had thought were nothing but characters in fiction until people found out vampires and their hunters were real.

The rings Jeliyah took from the pouch and put on her fingers all hummed softly. One ring on each finger, including her thumbs, and two bracelets, one for each wrist.

"Nice hardware. Planning to punch the rogue?"

Jeliyah met his gaze as she pulled her gun and leveled it at Teaghan's feet. "Activate." The gun hummed like the rings she wore. "The rings allow me to turn any gun or metal weapon I use into a necrome weapon. I happen to be ambidextrous."

Teaghan whistled under his breath. Vampires moved too fast for bullets. Most vampires only dodged far enough to avoid being hit, preferring to let the projectile skim past them to show the shooter how useless the weapon was. Close vicinity to a necrome bullet would cause pain and eventual paralysis. Maybe he wouldn't have to babysit this necromancer after all. "Ready?"

She nodded.

"Good. Where is he?" Teaghan turned toward the woods.

Jeliyah moved to his side. With her free hand, she rubbed the necrome hanging around her neck. "Locate." She looked one way and then the other before saying, "There are three vampires in the woods. Two with markers and one without. The one without is skirting the perimeter in—" she pointed to the left "—that direction."

"Fuck. Move your ass, necromancer. Some others are after my payday." He ran forward but kept his pace slow so he wouldn't lose Jeliyah, which was the last reason he hated necromancers—they ran too slow. "Keep an eye on the markers. Let me know when they get close."

Two others on the same hunt meant an accident might happen. And by accident, he meant someone shooting him in the back to make sure he didn't get the rogue before them. Enforcers weren't the work-together type. Few people were when money was involved. But those other two had the same problem as Teaghan— they each had necromancers slowing them down.

He glanced over his shoulder and saw Jeliyah keeping pace with him. He sped up and so did she. Good. At least she could run. And the way her tits bounced every time her feet struck the ground was nice too. Oh yeah, he definitely liked this necromancer better than the ones in the past.

CHAPTER

TWO

If Teaghan continued looking over his shoulder and grinning at her like that, Jeliyah was going to shoot him in the back. Her trigger finger twitched. She told herself it was because of the necromes humming and not because she was considering firing on her partner.

A rip was one thing. That punishment had a time limit. Heading back to campus after injuring her enforcer without justification—self-defense was always excusable—was a punishment no necromancer wanted. That meant being presented to the vampires, who were given permission to do whatever they wanted to the necromancer until the slight was satisfied. It was a one-way street from which no one had ever returned.

Jeliyah didn't know anyone in recent memory who had warranted such a punishment, but she'd heard the visiting alumni's anecdotes of what they had witnessed—probably more horror stories to scare the underclassmen into behaving. Even if they exaggerated, there had to be some truth, which made the punishment something Jeliyah didn't want happening to her.

Two glowing white dots in her peripheral vision were closing in on their position. Her tracking map, which was a mental image of the surrounding area and the vampires in it imposed over her regular vision, worked better with her eyes closed while she was in a stationary position, but that wasn't an option.

In a low whisper, she said, "Markers incoming. Two and five."

Teaghan glanced in the directions she'd indicated but didn't stop running. "How fast?"

"Human speed."

"Slower than us?"

"A little under."

"Where's the rogue?"

Jeliyah shifted her gaze to the lone red dot, which changed the orientation of the map and made her a little dizzy. Hence why it was better to use the map with her eyes closed while stationary. At least she didn't stumble.

The red dot hadn't moved. Was the rogue waiting for them? That was ballsy of him. Or maybe rogues did stuff like that. "Twelve o'clock. We're closest."

"So the markers are coming after us." Amusement tinged Teaghan's voice.

Jeliyah didn't know why he found that funny. Enforcer infighting was one of the first things necromancers learned about once they started training to be in the field. Lesson number one—stay out of it.

Necromancers were forbidden to hurt an enforcer unless that enforcer was attacking them. If the enforcers attacked each other, the necromancers had to let them go at it without interfering. Jeliyah didn't feel like witnessing the vampire version of a pissing contest.

She stopped running and faced the position of the closest team.

Teaghan came back to her. "What the fuck, woman?"

"Shut it. I'm helping you like I'm supposed to." She holstered her gun and then reached out to him. "Give me your hand."

"Why?"

"Hurry up, vampire. You're the one bitching about a payday. Now give me your damn hand." She knew why he was hesitating. Necro-metal hurt vampires—directed at them or not. But it was supposed to be equal to getting burned by a match, painful but not lasting. Well, not lasting so long as the contact was brief. If she held him too long, he would lose use of his arm as the magic of the necromes negated the magic that animated him.

Teaghan slapped his hand against hers and grimaced. She placed her other hand on top of his, concentrated her energy to cast a spell she'd only read about and then said, "Ghost Status."

The two white dots stopped advancing. Teaghan had dropped off their radar. The spell had worked. She'd masked Teaghan's marker—the magical beacon that denoted he was a hunter to other necromancers so they didn't attack him.

Satisfied with her achievement and a little winded, she released him. "You've got a few minutes of anonymity. Make them count."

He pulled his hand back and shook it. "Nice trick. Didn't know you necromancers could do that."

"Most can't. It takes too much energy." She would leave her explanation at that, since most necromancers couldn't because the campus didn't teach Ghost Status. Bent over and resting her palms on her knees, she was breathing hard as though she'd just run a one-minute mile. Casting Ghost Status was the magical equivalent. "I'm good for a Shield, maybe a Stun, for the next few hours, but that's about it. The rest is on you."

"I can deal." He swept her into his arms and took off running at vampire speed, which had to be close to forty miles per hour. Maybe slower because of the trees.

"What the hell?" Jeliyah had no choice but to hang on to him. If he dropped her now, the fall would break something, if not kill her outright.

"They can't see me, but you can still see them. Keep reporting their positions. The rogue too."

She closed her eyes and focused on the dots. The two other

enforcers were on the move again, faster this time. The rogue had left the perimeter and was heading straight for the house. Like she'd thought, ballsy. Maybe the rogue had been waiting around to see if someone would come to meet him.

She said, "The rogue is moving toward eleven. Cautious speed. I'd say a little above human. The enforcers are moving to intercept, still human speed."

"We'll get there first." His hold on her tightened, and he ran faster. The hand on her rib cage moved up so it nestled under her breast.

Jeliyah would have smacked him if he was using this position to cop a feel. The lecherous grin sitting on his face was a good indication he might be. This rogue better be worth it.

She would find out in a second. Teaghan stopped long enough to put her down and pull the sword he had strapped to his back—something that was at odds with his gangsta image.

Enforcers preferred swords and other edged weapons. Most vampires could move faster than a bullet, though that wasn't enough incentive for her to give up her gun. Plus, guns weren't great for close combat, which was always what these skirmishes turned into if prolonged.

Resting against the tree Teaghan had left her by, Jeliyah tried to make sense of the battle so she could jump in when needed. Teaghan and the rogue were moving too fast to track. All she caught were the sparks when their swords clashed.

There was one way to slow the rogue, but that meant removing Ghost Status on Teaghan's marker. Other necromancers couldn't see him, but she couldn't either. She could aim at the red dot, which was the rogue, but her spell would hit any other vampire in the vicinity as well. Her magic wouldn't target Teaghan so long as she knew where he was. Maintaining Ghost Status was taking a lot of energy. If she was going to take it down, she needed to do it now.

She glanced at the two marker dots. They were closer, but still far enough away that they shouldn't cause Teaghan any trouble. She would chance it.

Clasping her hands, she said, "Cancel." As she thought, the two markers paused for a second before speeding up their approach. She spread her hands toward the clashing swords and pushed her power through the necromes toward the red dot. "Halt."

The rogue stopped mid-swing as if he'd run into a wall. He looked her way, an expression of rage contorting his features. Teaghan lopped his head off with a single, quick slice and then caught the head while the body fell.

Teaghan looked at the head and then at Jeliyah. "What the fuck, woman? How the hell did you cast that without hitting me?"

Jeliyah slid down the tree to the ground, breathing hard again. She'd overestimated her ability to cast Halt so soon after Ghost Status, which meant Shield and Stun would have also been too much. She should have gone for Disarm or possibly Trip instead. In a breathy voice, she said, "Your previous necromancers must have been low-level golds if that impressed you."

If Teaghan had a reply, she didn't catch it because the world faded.

———

Teaghan sighed. Jeliyah's head drooped forward, and she sagged to the side. She'd fainted. He'd never had a partner do that. She'd overexerted herself, which meant she would be out of it for a few hours. This hunt was over, so it didn't bother him. If she pulled this shit in the middle of a hunt, he would beat her ass.

A grin curved his lips at the idea of yanking down her pants to reveal her round ass so he could smack it. He wouldn't stop until her skin glowed with the heat of blood rushing to the surface. But by then, she would beg for more. Jeliyah seemed like the type who would like a good spanking. But he would have to find that out later.

He pulled a plastic bag out of his back pocket, stuffed the head inside, looped the handles over his wrist and then picked up Jeliyah. She draped over his arms with her neck bared. If he had been any other type of vampire, that would have been a nice invitation.

The electric shocks of pain slicing up his arms and his incoming company curbed the thought. Most necromes went inactive when the user lost consciousness. Not so with Jeliyah's. Hers were shielding her like stinging nettles. He'd gotten himself quite a powerful partner this time around.

Ignoring the pain and hugging her close so her head rested on his shoulder, Teaghan ran at top speed back to his car. He didn't have time or the inclination to deal with the other two enforcers. His marker had tagged the head as his kill—something those in charge had quickly come up with to curtail stealing kills—so they wouldn't try to take it. But he didn't feel like dealing with the posturing and warnings about staying off their turf... as if it belonged to them.

That territorial crap was for the head families. Enforcers went where the money was. A few enforcers tried to stake a claim on an area, but they spent more time fighting with other enforcers to keep it than bringing in bounties. Teaghan and the rest of the majority believed in the snooze-and-lose way of doing things.

Jeliyah sighed in her sleep and then spoke soundless words. Her lips brushed his neck in light caresses that made Teaghan's dick jump to attention. He stumbled at the instant reaction but regained his footing before he hit a tree.

Less than a day with this woman and she already had him reacting to her briefest touch. That made up Teaghan's mind. Jeliyah was going to be in his bed sooner rather than later. He just had to convince her of that fact... and get her to ditch the necromes.

The tingling had lessened since she started speaking. Whatever she dreamed about, she must feel safe. He hoped it stayed that way, at least while he was holding her. The last thing he needed was her activating these stupid things because of a nightmare. He'd been on the wrong end of a necrome before, back in his rebellious days. He didn't feel like repeating the experience.

The car came in sight and he slowed his speed. On the passenger side, he shuffled Jeliyah's weight to one arm so he could grab her duffel bag and toss it out of the way. He lowered her to the seat and then fastened her seat belt. After retrieving her duffel bag, he shoved it and the severed head in the trunk. It was a tight fit with his bag also stashed in the back, but there was no other place for it. The trunk closed, and that's all he cared about.

He hopped into the driver's seat and glanced at Jeliyah. She was smiling about something. His dick twitched. She looked better with a smile. He would bet she looked fantastic with those plump lips open and moaning her pleasure.

Teaghan started the car and peeled out of the lot, headed for the nearest motel. The first sign he saw that said cable TV, laundry service, and free breakfast was where he stopped to get a room.

His cell played a hip-hop beat just as he was laying Jeliyah on one of the two double beds. She frowned in her sleep and her necromes glowed, forming a shield around her that crackled with the energy powering it.

Timing. Teaghan stepped back from the bed and answered his phone. "What?"

"Yo, Big T. It's Rick. You busy?"

"Not so much. What you got for me?"

"The usual. Three large for the night plus tips. You in?"

"Where?"

"Kent's."

Teaghan shook his head. "Five plus tips and free drinks."

"Come on, man. You're killing me."

"Take it or leave it. I just came off a hunt, so I'm happy to take my ass to bed. And for putting up with Kent's bullshit, I should charge you an extra three instead of two. I'm giving you a discount on account of me being in a good mood."

"Fine. Fine. Five, tips, and drinks. When can you get here?"

"Give me an hour. I've got to cash out." He ended the call and clipped the phone back in its holster.

He perused Jeliyah's body, lingering at her breasts. "Damn shame."

He would have liked to stay and see how far he could get with his little partner, but her necromes activating had stalled that idea. The woman must have a real hate on for hip-hop to react in her sleep like that to a little music. If he tried to touch her now, the shield surrounding her would send enough voltage through him to make a lightning rod jealous.

Since he wasn't a masochist or the suicidal type, he decided to leave his exploration for another night, preferably one where she wasn't wearing those damn necromes. Though he would be limited to exploring until she gave him permission to do more.

He grinned at the thought of how he would get that permission. Her breasts would be his first stop. He wanted to spend time getting to know those twin mounds until Jeliyah was pleading for him to do more. And she would. Teaghan hadn't met a woman yet who didn't ask for more once he got started.

His phone went off again. Jeliyah's barrier intensified, casting the entire room in blue light. He shook his head as he answered the call. "What?"

"You free, Teag?"

Speaking of begging. "Not tonight. I'm at Kent's."

"Shit. I knew that bastard would get to you first. Fine. I want you for the rest of the week."

"You got me, Lee. Hunts take precedence."

"Always. I know the deal. Three, tips, drinks?"

"Three, tips, drinks, and a guest."

"You're bringing a guest? That's a first. Never thought you would get serious about someone."

"She's my partner."

"I thought you hated your partners."

"This one is fast changing my mind."

"Got you down for a guest. Tomorrow then." The phone clicked as the call ended.

Teaghan decided his phone going off was a good thing. Jeliyah's shield meant he could leave and not worry about her being attacked. Not that he had been too worried about it when he took the job. No one would have tracked him that fast, and the report had said there was only one rogue in the area.

He hung the *Do Not Disturb* sign on the knob on his way out. Jeliyah probably wouldn't wake before he got back. If she did, she should be able to figure out the deal with no explanation needed. Not that he expected her to miss him, not yet. Once he got her addicted to all the pleasure he could give her, that's when the missing would start. That's when he would get rid of her because he hated clingy women, which was what they all became when they got thoughts of love mixed in the fucking.

He hopped into his car and checked the surrounding area for anything suspicious. Everything appeared normal. He started the car, gunned the engine a few times, and then peeled out of the parking lot. His thoughts went to the many women who had helped him hone his bedroom skills over the centuries. Each relationship had ended on bad terms since Teaghan had cut the women loose when they started in on the forever-after talk.

Needy women turned nosy and nagging, which graduated to interfering with his business. But that was a few months away, at least. Jeliyah would take time to come around. He knew that already. Once she got to the becoming-a-pain-in-the-ass stage, Teaghan should be close to retiring her, which solved the problem nicely. Retired necromancers didn't stay in the field. They couldn't.

He didn't know what necromancers did after they ended their partnerships with him. They called it retirement, and he hadn't bothered to ask. He knew no able-bodied necromancer would be allowed to take the money and go off to some tropical island somewhere. Necromancers were too rare for that. Retirement was code for something else. Something desirable that cost a lot of money. Money Teaghan was on his way to get.

He parked the car at the curb outside a three-story red-brick building with a wrought-iron gate for a door. The two enforcers standing on either side of that door nodded to Teaghan as he neared them. He returned the nod before pulling the door open and entering the building.

The smell of burning torches greeted his nose. No fluorescents or other type of artificial light in the reserve. It was vampire owned and managed, so everything was firelight—candle chandeliers, wall torches, and lanterns. Though it wasn't as though a vampire needed much light. The whole place could be pitch black, and the vampires would be fine. The few humans who worked there needed the light, though.

Teaghan walked to the first open teller and placed the bagged severed head on the counter. "Rogue seven-seven-five-three-eight."

"I thought you got pulled off that hunt to meet your new partner," the teller, a human Teaghan had dealt with many times in the past, said as he slid the head closer and opened the plastic bag. He peered at the head and then at his computer screen.

Teaghan said, "I did, and you all didn't waste time giving my hunt to someone else."

The teller shrugged his indifference. "The twins were on the premises when you got yanked. It looks bad for them that you managed to get sidetracked for—what?—an hour and still got the kill before them."

"My new partner is good at her job."

"Or the twins suck at theirs. Either way, the payday is yours." The man re-wrapped the head and carried it to a back room. When he returned, he held a palm-sized pouch. He plopped it on a black velvet-covered tray, which he slid across the counter.

Teaghan upended the pouch contents onto the tray. Several

pinky-nail-sized jewels spilled out and sparkled in the light. Rubies, emeralds, and sapphires. Teaghan didn't take diamonds as payment. The value fluctuated too much for his liking.

He held each gem up to the light and examined the quality. The reserve wasn't above passing off low-quality gems to those too stupid to check or know what they were looking for. He placed one sapphire on the counter beside the tray and flicked it with his finger, sending the jewel flying past the teller's shoulder like a bullet from a gun. It embedded in the wall behind the man.

Teaghan said, "Try again."

The teller didn't flinch. He left and came back with a new sapphire that he dropped on Teaghan's open palm. He said, "I don't put the payments together. I just deliver them."

Teaghan checked the gem before putting it with the others. "And I'm not above punishing the messenger. You know to check my shit before you bring it to me." He scooped the gems back into the pouch, tied off the top, and then dropped the pouch into his pants pocket, which he zipped closed. "You got my number when the next rogue shows."

"Yup, we do. Good night, Teaghan."

He didn't return the farewell as he left the building. Another enforcer carrying a plastic-wrapped head was coming in as Teaghan was leaving. He might have promised a week to Lee, but Teaghan harbored no illusions he could do all the nights. The rogue counts had gotten high the last few months, and the head family wasn't saying why.

They didn't need to. Teaghan knew the beginnings of a war when he saw one. The enforcers would be working their asses off to keep the humans from figuring it out. The last thing the vampire nation needed was the humans interfering in something that was none of their business.

The head families clashed from time to time, even the United States families who pretended to work together when the humans were looking. The rogue Teaghan had taken out tonight wasn't foreign, and he hadn't been an assassin either. If Teaghan had to guess, he'd killed a scout—a sacrificial lamb sent to test the defenses. That would explain why the rogue had been standing around waiting for an attack.

If things were going the way Teaghan knew they were, his little necromancer might be retiring earlier than they both thought.

CHAPTER

THREE

Jeliyah came awake with a loud gasp, bolting to a sitting position. She looked around in confusion. Where was she? A motel room? It resembled a motel room with the two side-by-side beds separated by a nightstand, across from a TV sitting on a dresser.

"Morning, sleeping beauty," Teaghan said from the doorway. He tossed a small pouch her way. "That's your half."

She caught it and pulled it open, revealing the various jewels within—the usual form of payment for rogue kills. Vampires had lived long enough to see monetary systems come and go. They didn't trust them. All their transactions were in jewels and precious metals.

"Half?" She looked up at Teaghan, who sat on the other bed. "I thought necromancers got less than that." It had always bothered her that a necromancer's partner issued payment. Teaghan could have tossed her a couple dollars, and she wouldn't be allowed to complain. Or she could but no one would listen. A low wage kept her from retirement, which was in the campus's best interest.

"You did half the work, you get half the pay. With me, necromancers get paid based on the work they do. Most necromancers I've had toss out a Shield or two and call it a day. That's the fastest rogue takedown I've had in a long while." His gaze wandered over her before returning to her face. "Why is a high class like you slumming it with the enforcers? Shouldn't you be with the big boys guarding someone with too much money and not enough to spend it on?"

Jeliyah clutched the bag and said in a low voice, "I'm not high class. I'm palladium level, which is just below." If she'd were platinum level, she wouldn't have been dreaming of being partnered with an enforcer and eventual retirement.

Platinum levels dreamed of secret service detail, the richer and more powerful the client the better. A couple of platinum levels had been hired by one of the vampire families to guard a parliament member. That had been a huge scandal when it happened—necromancers playing bodyguards for a vampire. But the vampire had paid the asking price, so they were in his employ.

According to the rumors, that family didn't bother with enforcers and had ousted all the ones they used to have. No rogue was dumb enough to attack a vampire with platinum level necromancers watching his back. No one in the family was dumb enough to challenge for his position either.

She said, "No matter how strong I am, I'm still palladium level. I don't get guard duty." She sighed with a shake of her head. "Passing out after casting Ghost Status and then Halt. No platinum level would be that weak."

"Weak or not, you got the job done without having me save your ass. That's already five times better than everyone before you."

"You must have pissed off Hirsch if you've been getting such weak necromancers. Most of his precinct are rose gold and white gold with a few palladiums, like me. I think I've only seen a few yellow gold and maybe one or two silver come through the door since I arrived." All of whom had gotten partners before her, but she kept that bit to herself.

Teaghan rubbed his chin in thought. "I might have told him to suck my left nut sac on more than one occasion." He grinned and met her gaze. "And he wasn't happy when he found me sleeping with his wife."

"That was you?"

"Heard about it, did you?"

"Hirsch spent an entire month last year bitching about nothing else after his wife left him and took their daughter with her. I heard they went to shack up with some vampire."

"Not me. I had my fun and moved on. She must have gotten a taste and decided vampire was the way to go."

"Idiot."

"Don't knock it unless you've tried it, sweetness." He licked his lips as he gave her another languid perusal. "I'm more than willing to break you off a piece of what she got. Just say when."

"So very not interested, and it's against policy for necromancers and enforcers to fraternize." She looked him up and down. "Even if I did decide to ignore policy, it wouldn't be for some confused white boy like you."

"Confused about what?"

"Have you looked in a mirror?"

"Often. I look damn good, if I do say so myself."

"Keep telling yourself that." She moved to the other side of the bed and stood up. "Where's my bag? Where are we? And did you say morning?"

"Bag's in the corner. We're at a motel. And what's it look like to you?" He pulled aside the curtain, letting bright sunlight spill into the room.

Jeliyah shielded her eyes until he let the curtain fall back into place. She'd slept all night and into the day. Not good. Recuperating shouldn't have taken that long, overexertion or not.

She got off the bed and went in the direction Teaghan had pointed, retrieving the pouch where she kept her necromes and started removing them. Of course Teaghan wouldn't have done it. He couldn't.

Once in place, only the necromancer could remove them. The exception to that being death and then they became inactive so a vampire could touch them without harm. The only necrome she left in place was the one around her neck. That was one she never removed. It had been her first, fashioned after a charm she'd seen in a store.

Teaghan said, "Finally. You were glowing like a beacon when I left."

"Glowing?" She looked down at herself. "My shields were up all night?" That would explain why it had taken her so long to regain consciousness. She'd been expending energy as fast as she recovered it. She must have felt threatened and activated her shield.

What had Teaghan done after she passed out that she felt the need? Then the other thing he said registered. "What do you mean, left? Left where?"

"Work, sweetness."

"You did a rogue hunt without me?"

"Bounty hunting isn't my only source of income. It pays, but I'm not about to sit on my ass waiting for another idiot with a death wish."

Some feeling told her not to ask, so she heeded it and didn't. Instead, she waved her hand at their surroundings. "Why a motel? Don't you have a house?" She'd been prepared to be his houseguest. It was standard practice for necromancers to stay with their enforcer partners. When a call for a hunt came in, retrieving people wasted time, so the partners became roommates until the assignment ended.

"Bed, TV, and a laundry room. That's all I need. And why waste money on a house I'll never see and that might potentially get attacked?"

There was that. Rogues didn't always go after the head families.

Sometimes they went after enforcers—taking out the sentries before going after their primary target. Having a house made an enforcer easy to find.

She asked, "Then why not a better motel than this? A hotel even? With all that gold hanging around your neck, I would think you could afford a nicer room."

"Bed, TV, and a laundry room. Everything else is superfluous and superficial. It's only a few nights. Get over it. You can pick where we sleep next time. Anything over fifty a night and you're paying the difference."

Jeliyah couldn't argue with his logic. "Fine. You said a few nights, so that means we're moving motels again?"

"After every hunt. Safer that way."

Again, sound logic.

"This place also has breakfast, except you missed it." He kicked off his shoes and lay down. "I'm getting some sleep. Whatever you plan to do, do it quietly."

Jeliyah almost snorted. Sleep. Vampires didn't sleep. They died. Time of day didn't matter since sunlight did nothing to them except irritate their eyes.

A vampire's body shut down when they slept—no breathing, no heartbeat, nothing. Many a past hunter had been killed because they mistook a vampire for a corpse and ignored them until it was too late.

She had no intention of killing Teaghan... yet... but it would be interesting to see a sleeping vampire up close. "Before you drop off, can I borrow your car?"

"No."

"I need to run a few errands."

"You need to learn to catch the bus. And leave your cell number. If I get a call for a hunt, I want to know how to find you."

Except she didn't have one. That was one of the errands. She hadn't needed one. Jeliyah's life had been the office and her tiny apartment, which she'd closed out the second she learned she was getting a partner. She would have gotten a phone then, but there hadn't been enough time between notification and the first meeting.

She scribbled out a list of what she needed and then took a quick shower. Teaghan was out when she exited the bathroom. Vampires had to go dormant for a certain amount of time each day, or they aged and eventually deteriorate. The period of dormancy differed from vampire to vampire, like human sleep patterns. It was literally beauty sleep.

A vampire not allowed to rest turned into a skeletal husk, but that took weeks—if not months—and made them more dangerous. Blood could restore them. The rate of deterioration determined how much blood they needed. The worse off they were, the more they craved blood and attacked anything with a pulse to get it.

Teaghan needed sleep, and she needed food.

Jeliyah left the room and headed for the nearest fast-food place with a decent menu. After that, she would head to the closest parcel service store to get a mailbox, and then to the bank to get a safe-deposit box for her pouch of jewels. She wouldn't cash them in all at once. One or two would pad her bank account while the rest would wait for her to need them.

It was almost sundown before she returned to the motel room. Teaghan opened his eyes the second she closed the door.

She said with amusement, "I thought it was only a stereotype that vampires slept all day."

"Vampires are, by nature, nocturnal. I slept all day because I was working all night, like I'll be doing tonight."

"Working doing what?"

He grinned as he sat up. "I DJ at the local clubs."

Jeliyah rolled her eyes and shook her head. How much more of a cliché could he be? "Have fun."

"You're coming with."

"No, I'm not."

He stood and loomed over her. "Yes, you are."

"You don't frighten me."

He grinned, flashing his gold-capped fang as he stepped close enough that she could feel his body heat. "Your accelerated heart rate says otherwise, necromancer."

"I'm not used to being around a vampire. That's all."

"All the more reason to come with. The club has a whole host of vampires. You can get over your shyness." He grabbed her wrist and dragged her behind him out of the room and down to the car.

Jeliyah was seated in the passenger seat with Teaghan driving them downtown before she had time to argue. Hanging around a loud club was not the way she'd planned to spend her night. Actually, she had no clue how she had planned to spend her night, but at a club had been nowhere on the list.

Teaghan pulled the car into a crowded parking lot next to a repurposed warehouse with a line of waiting people wrapped around the exterior. A few people pointed his way and started waving. Was he some sort of celebrity? Jeliyah curbed the inclination to ask. She didn't care if he was.

"Take it off." Teaghan pointed at the necrome around her neck.

She grasped it between two fingers in a defensive gesture. "No."

"This club is predominately vampires. You'll cause trouble walking in with that thing around your neck."

"Not if I don't go."

"You're already here. Now take it off."

Jeliyah hadn't taken off the necrome since her trainer put it on her ten years ago. It was her first necrome. She wouldn't feel right not wearing it.

"Now."

With shaking fingers, she undid the clasp and removed the necklace. The necrome stopped humming the second it no longer touched her skin. She missed the familiar sound already.

Teaghan opened the glove box. He pulled out his shades and slipped them on.

"Shades?"

"Strobe lights." He pointed to the glove box. "In and let's go."

She laid the necrome inside and then had to yank her hand back to keep Teaghan from slamming her fingers in the closing door. "Watch it, vampire."

"It's a hunk of metal, not your fucking baby. Get over it." He hopped the car door and started walking to the club.

She followed him, glancing over her shoulder at the car every few steps. Teaghan didn't lock his car, and he left the top down. Would her necrome be safe? Necro-metal had no value except to a necromancer, but someone might steal it, thinking it was valuable.

She started to ask Teaghan if he could secure his car, but a flock of women surrounded him, cutting off her words.

He laughed and gave the giggling women each a kiss before ushering them into the club. She heaved a sigh as she followed.

Teaghan pointed her out to the doorman, who appeared a little surprised but nodded.

Jeliyah didn't know what the man's reaction meant and ignored him and the people waiting behind the velvet rope as she entered the club.

Loud music and thumping bass that beat her heart for her greeted Jeliyah. She was already tired and annoyed and she'd just gotten there. Moving close to Teaghan, she asked loud enough to be heard, "How do you vampires stand such loud music?"

"Earplugs." He jabbed his finger at his ear. Sure enough, he had a neon-green earplug stuffed in his ear.

"Why even go to a club if you're just going to wear earplugs? Doesn't that defeat the purpose?"

"We can still hear the music and everything else. The earplugs make it less piercing. It's about human volume."

"Oh."

One of the women hanging on Teaghan glared at Jeliyah before asking, "Who's she, Big T?"

He said, "She's in need of a new outfit. Do something about

that, sweet thang." He smacked the woman's ass, making her squeak and then giggle.

Jeliyah bristled. "I don't need—"

"Sure thing, Big T." The woman laid a kiss on his lips, making sure her breasts and the rest of her pressed against Teaghan before she turned to Jeliyah. "Come on." Her voice held a note of annoyance.

Teaghan said, "Pick something I like, Nessa." He winked at Jeliyah and then turned his back on her as he led the flock of women to the DJ booth. The man occupying the spot bumped fists with Teaghan before vacating.

"I said *come on*," Nessa snapped. "Damn."

Jeliyah glared at her but caught up with the woman as they walked to the back of the club. She didn't know why she followed Nessa or why she was at the club. It was a nice change of pace, though. Jeliyah decided to chalk it up to a new experience and go along with it.

Or that was her plan until she saw the dress Nessa pulled out of the closet. The woman held up a gray tube. "There you go. Big T will love this."

"Where's the rest of it?"

"This is it."

"What about pants?"

"This is a dress. You don't need pants."

"That's an oversized headband. I'm not wearing it."

"Big T said—"

"I don't give a damn what Teaghan said. I'm not wearing that."

Nessa sucked her teeth and rolled her eyes. "Fine." She dug through the closet and pulled out a one-legged catsuit. "What about this?"

The cut would leave Jeliyah's upper thigh exposed along with much of her waist, which meant no panties. "No."

She vetoed three more suggestions before giving in to the tube dress—a description she still didn't think fit. It stretched to

34

accommodate her curves, but stopped right below her ass. That wasn't long enough for her and requests for leggings got ignored.

Nessa led Jeliyah back to the DJ booth and Teaghan, who bopped his head to the music as he gave Jeliyah a once-over complete with licking his tongue over his gold canine and sucking his teeth. He grinned. "That's better."

"This isn't my normal style." Jeliyah pulled the back of the micro-minidress down, not liking the draft she felt on her upper thighs. The dress rode back up as soon as she released it.

Teaghan leaned to the side so he could look behind her. "It should be."

"Who asked you?" She yanked the dress down again and held it. "Pay attention to your music, vampire."

He laughed but returned to mixing music.

Jeliyah hugged the back wall, refusing to go into the crowd with her ass exposed. The women around Teaghan ignored her. Good. She was there, which satisfied Teaghan. He wasn't making her do anything besides be there, which satisfied her.

She wished she had a pair of Teaghan's earplugs but settled on trying to drown out the music by reciting spells in her head.

The night would be over soon.

CHAPTER
FOUR

Jeliyah hated to admit it but Teaghan did his job well. The music was good and kept the crowd in high energy the whole night. It ended with him getting a bite to eat from the women who'd stayed by his side the entire time. Each one propositioned him, touching his thighs and crotch and rubbing their barely covered breasts against him, but he turned them all down.

On the way to the car, Jeliyah asked, "So you work for blood then?"

Teaghan held out his arms. "Do I look like I'm holding a sign that says *'will work for food'*? No, sweetness, I work for cash. Lee, the owner, gave me mine after you left to get dressed. DJs get paid a wage, tips, and sometimes free drinks. The girls are drinks."

"They're more than that." Jeliyah couldn't keep the edge of disgust out of her voice.

"Depends on my mood and theirs." Teaghan grinned at her. "Jealous?"

"You wish."

"You do—"

Jeliyah blinked as Teaghan went flying backward. His actions made no sense until she realized Teaghan had been sucker-punched by a large, cro-mag-looking man. Said man turned his sights on Jeliyah. She didn't have time to scream before he tackled her to the ground and wrapped his hands around her throat, choking her.

He laughed, spraying her with his spit. "Die, you necromancer bitch."

A vampire. She could see his fangs now that he had his mouth open. If she had her necrome, she would have known that from the start. Not having it also meant she had no way to defend herself.

Her rings were back at the motel. Her necklace was in the car. Damn Teaghan and his stupid side job. If she died, she planned to haunt him for the rest of his days, keeping him awake so he shriveled into a pile of dust.

"Jeliyah!" Teaghan's yell drew her attention.

Something glinted overhead. She could feel the hum of the necro-metal and reached out to it with her magic. Having no time for anything fancy and not touching the metal to guide the magic meant anything she cast would hit Teaghan and any other vampire in the immediate vicinity, as well. She croaked, "Repel."

The vampire above her grunted as a wall of energy blew him away from her and sent him flying across the parking lot.

Teaghan grunted and then cursed.

Jeliyah sat up in time to see him land near the other man. They both pulled swords and then blurred out of view. Jeliyah busied herself looking for her necrome. She'd heard it land, but the dark parking lot made it hard to find.

The headlights of a passing car reflected off the metal, and Jeliyah grabbed it. She didn't bother putting on the necklace. Holding the necrome in a tight fist, she said, "Activate."

Two white dots entered her field of vision. Jeliyah stared at them. Another enforcer? Why was another enforcer attacking her? Enforcers—in fact, all vampires—knew a necromancer on sight, necro-metal accessories or not. It was the magic the necromancers possessed. A new vampire might have the excuse of ignorance, but not an enforcer.

Jeliyah started to call a warning to Teaghan that he was fighting another enforcer, when the two men stopped and faced each other.

Teaghan sneered at his opponent. "Which one are you? Dumas or Didios? I could never tell you fuckers apart."

"Didios. You took our hunt."

"Correction—you got called to take my hunt, and I took it back. And that issue pales compared to you attacking my necromancer. You've gone rogue, Didios. That means your ass is mine." Teaghan lunged forward with his sword in front of him.

Jeliyah watched the dots because the men themselves were all but invisible to her. Even the dots moved too fast to follow at times. She couldn't help. Her partnership with Teaghan hadn't been long enough to know his distinct marker. She couldn't tell the men apart, so anything she cast would hit both. But she couldn't stand around doing nothing.

Her mind rushed as she tried to think of all the different spells she knew. She needed something that would hinder and help at the same time, but that she could also cast with only her amulet. It was a defense necrome. Her rings were for fighting. Teaghan and his stupid clubbing.

Defense.

Of course!

Jeliyah summoned up her power and focused on Shield. With a push and a prayer, she trapped one dot and hoped it was the one she wanted.

Didios came back into view when his sword bounced off the invisible barrier surrounding Teaghan.

"Necromancers. Never leave home without them." Teaghan smirked as he thrust his sword through Didios's chest and then yanked it sideways, cutting the man's heart in half. He brought his sword around and severed Didios's head from his shoulders.

Jeliyah lowered the shield before rushing forward.

Teaghan wiped his sword on Didios's clothes, then sheathed it. "Good job."

"Not really," she rasped, her throat scratchy from being choked. "I was hoping to put him in the shield, not you."

"What good would that have done? Trying to kill me off, necromancer? And here I thought we were getting along."

"Shield can keep people out or hold them in. I planned to catch him to limit his movement. When I saw it landed on you, I switched it from confinement to protection."

"Quick thinking and smart. Nice to know you have brains and beauty."

She shrugged, trying not to let his compliment go to her head. "It's all I could think to do. I don't know your marker. I couldn't tell you two apart—and what the hell? Why did he attack me?"

Teaghan yanked a plastic bag from one of his pants pockets and stashed Didios's head in it. "Pissed that we took his hunt last night. I'm guessing the twins are hard up if one went rogue and attacked you. He knew that was a death sentence. Only someone desperate—or really dumb—would do it."

"Both?"

"With the twins, that's a high possibility." He unclipped his cell phone and hit the speed dial before putting it to his ear. "Yeah, this is Teaghan. I need a cleanup at Sugar-Sugar downtown."

Jeliyah looked at Didios's body. His blood seeped out, staining the parking lot. In a few hours, no one would know he'd been killed there. The cleanup crews the vampires sent were good at their jobs, but then they'd been cleaning up vampire corpses for centuries so humans never found them.

She asked, "Are you going to get in trouble? He did attack me, but Didios hadn't been declared a rogue and he's an enforcer."

"He's dead and that bruise around your neck is all the proof I need for the kill. Come on." Teaghan walked away.

Jeliyah followed him to his car and was a little surprised when he held the door open for her. She got in, settled herself, and then reached for the head. Teaghan pulled it back while he closed the door. He put the head in the trunk. Jeliyah decided not to question it since she hadn't wanted to hold it.

Teaghan drove them to the reserve. It was her first time going there. She'd never thought she would. Enforcers rarely brought necromancers to the vampire bank. The only humans allowed inside were the ones who worked there, and those were few and far between.

At the door, Teaghan glared down the guards when they started to bar Jeliyah's way. He put his arm around her waist and yanked her against his side as they entered. The enforcers followed them inside and up to the teller Teaghan chose to receive Didios's head.

The teller didn't look at the bag and continued staring at his computer screen with a bored—or maybe it was fed-up—manner. He clicked his mouse with a sigh. "You weren't assigned a hunt."

"This fucker attacked my necromancer. I took him out."

The teller turned his gaze to Jeliyah. "Necromancer?"

She nodded, then hissed at the pain in her throat. Her voice still rasped when she said, "No provocation. We think he was pissed that Teaghan took his hunt."

"It happens," the man said with an indifferent shrug. He opened the plastic bag. "Yup, that's one of the twins, all right."

"Teaghan." Jeliyah and Teaghan faced Fredrick, the vampire who had accompanied Teaghan the day before. The man nodded to them in greeting. "Good timing. I was about to call you with a hunt."

Teaghan said, "Let me guess. Dumbass and Dipshit."

"Their names are Dumas and Didios. And how did you know I was calling you about the twins?"

"Because I already solved half the problem." Teaghan jerked his thumb over his shoulder at the teller and the bag in front of him.

Fredrick went to the counter and pulled down the edge of the bag. "I only just authorized this hunt."

"Next time, how about you authorize it before he goes after my partner, so I have a little warning?"

"He went after the necromancer?"

Teaghan gestured to Jeliyah's neck as his answer.

"Then it wasn't isolated." Fredrick closed the bag and pushed it at the teller. "Pay the man."

The teller picked up the bag and walked away.

Jeliyah asked, "What's not isolated? Did he attack someone else before coming after me?"

"His necromancer. It's the reason I changed their status to rogue. We got an emergency call from Dumas's necromancer that Didios had killed his own. The call got cut short. We're not sure if the other necromancer is alive or not. Since neither twin works alone, we're assuming this insubordination is both of them and we gave them both rogue status."

Teaghan released Jeliyah when the teller returned with the payment. He checked each jewel with quick, precise movements and then handed the bag to Jeliyah. He asked Fredrick, "Dead or alive?"

"The necromancers want him alive for interrogation. The head family wants him dead."

"Which one is paying the highest?"

Fredrick grinned. "How mercenary of you."

"Me and every other enforcer, or we wouldn't be doing this job. Which one?"

"The family is prepared to pay ten percent above anything the necromancers will offer."

"Dead it is." Teaghan slipped his arm around Jeliyah's waist again and escorted her out of the building. They were in the car, headed back to the motel, when Teaghan asked, "No lectures about how I should capture Dumas alive and hand him over to the necromancers?"

"You don't know me well enough to assume I would say something like that. If the trustees want him, they'll send a team

41

after him. That they left it up to an enforcer means it's lip service. The necromancers want him dead as much as the head family does. But they know the families of the murdered necromancers will want answers, so they act like they want Dumas alive to placate them."

"And they call vampires shady."

"Also, the necromancers get an enforcer to do a job while sticking the head family with the bill. Not to mention, the head family will owe restitution to the partners' families for ordering a kill when the necromancers wanted him alive. That restitution will probably be in the amount of both men's retirements, plus a little extra for the families."

"Cash rules everything around me."

"Cream."

Teaghan grinned at her. "Know that song, do you?"

"I don't dislike hip-hop."

"Oh, so it's me you don't like."

"I thought we'd already established that."

Silence descended for the rest of the ride back to the motel.

Teaghan walked Jeliyah to the room door with his hand on the small of her back. She didn't know why he felt the need to keep touching her. She also didn't know why she didn't call an end to it.

He said, "Pack. We're leaving."

"Okay. Here." She held the bag of jewels out to him.

"That's yours."

"What? All of it?"

"And half the next one when I kill Dumas. Get packed and meet me at the car. I'm going to check out." Teaghan grabbed his duffel bag and left the room.

Jeliyah stared after him in confusion. Why would he let her keep the entire payout and then promise her half of the next one? She knew she shouldn't look a gift horse in the mouth, but this day had gotten surreal.

Putting it out of her mind, she gathered up the few things she'd left spread around the room and shoved them back in her bag. In the next room, she would keep her belongings together. It seemed like Teaghan was the get-up-and-go type. She didn't want to slow him down.

To that end, she pulled her gun harness out and slipped into it. Didios had taught her a lesson about preparedness. She tied her pouch of necromes to the harness to have them close. That attack was the first and last time she would be so helpless.

She did one last walkthrough of the room for anything she might have overlooked before slinging her duffel onto her shoulder opposite her gun. Grabbing the bag of jewels, Jeliyah headed out of the room for Teaghan's car.

They would need to stop by her bank so she could stash the jewels in her safe deposit box, which is what she would tell Teaghan when he joined her. Or that was what she planned.

She didn't get a chance because he tackled her to the ground a few steps from his car. Gunshots rang out, stopping her from questioning his actions.

Teaghan pulled the motel room door shut and had to stop himself from leaning against it. There would be time to reflect on the night after they got to a new motel. Until then, he would hold off thinking about the way his heart had pounded when he caught sight of Jeliyah being choked. He also wouldn't let the urge to keep touching and holding her—assuring himself she was safe—make him reenter the room.

He went to the lobby to check out. The woman behind the counter gave him a fake smile while her eyes showed her disdain for his choice in clothing.

"Checking out. Room 115."

"Oh."

"What?"

"Nothing. Sorry." Her smile flipped from fake to real, and she blinked her eyes several times. "Did you enjoy your stay?"

"Fine. How much?" He didn't have time for this.

Not that he would have flirted with her if he had time. She wasn't his type. And she'd been less than interested in him until she caught sight of his canines. Vampire groupies were high on his list of women to avoid.

"Your total is eighty-seven dollars and sixty cents."

Teaghan flipped five twenties off the wad he'd gotten from Lee earlier and handed them to the clerk. DJing was the only time he accepted cash. The money wasn't much and it wouldn't last, so demanding jewels was a waste of time.

The woman took the bills from him, making sure her fingers brushed his. He let her touch him since snatching his hand away would cause drama he wanted to avoid.

The skin on the back of his neck crawled as someone with active necromes entered the vicinity. He'd told Jeliyah to wait at the car. Why had she come to the lobby?

The second the question entered his mind, he realized the sensation moving over his skin didn't feel familiar. Necromancers all had a feel unique to them—the magical equivalent of a fingerprint. After Jeliyah's barrier spell the night before, Teaghan knew her flavor well. This wasn't it. That meant another necromancer was near and had his necromes activated.

Teaghan ran from the lobby. The clerk called after him, but he ignored the woman. Dumas was here. Teaghan was sure of it. His necromancer was still alive, and Dumas was using the man to hunt Teaghan.

Teaghan cursed his marker and his own stupidity for forgetting it. But then, he'd never had to hide from a necromancer before, at least not since becoming an enforcer.

He caught sight of Jeliyah walking to the car at the same time he heard the shot. Teaghan dumped his duffel bag and put on speed to get to Jeliyah first. He slowed himself one second before he hit her so the impact wouldn't kill her, knocking her to the ground behind the car.

The bullet whizzed past her head, but several others followed it, aimed lower. Dumas was trying to hit them through the car. Teaghan would take the repair costs out of Dumas's ass before taking the man's head.

Teaghan sat up, assured the bullets wouldn't go through the car, and looked over at Jeliyah. "You hit?"

She felt her arms and chest before shaking her head. "No. You?"

"No."

"It's Dumas, right?"

"Has to be. I haven't pissed off anyone else but you this week."

The gunshots stopped.

Teaghan decided not to stick his head out and see why. Dumas might be waiting for that. And it seemed like Dumas wanted to take Teaghan out from a distance.

Of the two, Didios was the better close-combat fighter. Dumas was as good as dead when Teaghan found him.

He jabbed his finger at his shoulder where the marker was located. "Do something about this damn thing. It's how he's tracking me."

"So his necromancer is still alive then." Jeliyah rummaged through the pouch dangling from her gun harness. She quickly jammed her rings on and then grabbed his head. "Don't get any ideas from this."

He started to ask her what she meant, but her lips landing on his answered the question. Teaghan sat in stunned shock. He came back to his senses when Jeliyah bit his lower lip. She sucked at the wound, tasting his blood, and then he realized what she was doing —besides making him hard when he should be worried about killing the mofo who'd shot up his car.

Jeliyah pulled back from the kiss. Her upper lip and tongue were stained red with his blood. Her breath came in shudders and her grip on his head tightened as his blood entered her system, amping up her abilities.

She pulled in a deep breath and then said, "Activate. Recognize."

Teaghan's body hummed along with her necromes, but it wasn't painful or uncomfortable. The sensation could almost be described as soothing, like a tingling massage.

She shuddered again. "Confusion. Ghost Status."

"What's Confusion?"

Jeliyah dropped her hands from his head and hugged her arms. In a shaky voice, she said, "Decoys. It gives every vampire in a one-mile radius a beacon that mimics a marker."

"Nice." He stood. "You going to pass out again?"

She shook her head.

"You good on your own while I take care of him? We don't know if Dumas brought someone besides his necromancer."

Jeliyah slipped on her bracelets and then pulled out her gun. It started humming along with her necromes. Good enough for him.

Teaghan unsheathed his sword. Before he could walk away, Jeliyah said, "My necromes know you now. I can back you up from here without hitting you."

"Do it then. Where is he?"

She closed her eyes. "Chasing shadows. Headed for nine."

"Can you track his necromancer?"

"No."

"Keep me posted." He tapped his head and then ran after Dumas. There were a lot of vampires in this district. It was the other reason Teaghan chose motels here. A rogue wouldn't be able to pinpoint him. That was working in his favor with Dumas as well.

{You should see him. He's almost on top of you.} Jeliyah's telepathic voice entered Teaghan's head. She sounded as sweet as though she were whispering in his ear. *{Focus, vampire!}*

Teaghan was always focused, but that didn't stop him from

thinking about his blood inside Jeliyah. With it, her abilities were stronger and she could speak to him telepathically. It also meant she could read his thoughts... if he wasn't blocking her. She could see his surface thoughts, but nothing deeper. It was a one-way street unless he drank her blood.

{Not going to happen. Heads-up!}

"I see him," Teaghan said aloud as an answer to Jeliyah and to give Dumas a one- second warning before Teaghan swung his sword at the man's head. His sword hit a barrier, which deflected the sword and forced Teaghan back a few steps.

Dumas turned, grinned at him, and raised his gun. "I saw the way you killed my brother. I figured this would be poetic. After force-feeding the necromancer my blood, his Shield will withstand anything you and your necro-bitch toss at it." He started firing.

Teaghan dodged every shot, but he couldn't keep this up forever. A man standing off to the side caught his eye. The man had necro-metal bracers on both wrists—Dumas's partner, no doubt. He stood crying and appeared as though he wanted to run. So why didn't he?

"Don't even think of targeting my Renfield unless you plan to go rogue like me," Dumas said.

{Fuck.}

Teaghan echoed Jeliyah's sentiment. A necromancer turned Renfield—the slave of a vampire with no will of his own—was dangerous. So much more so than a necromancer who had tasted vampire blood. A Renfield-necromancer had the limitless energy of the vampire host to draw on, which meant Dumas's partner would outlast Jeliyah.

She said, {It also means the trustees will lock him away for the rest of his life if you manage to kill Dumas.}

"Not my issue, necromancer," Teaghan snapped as he deflected a bullet with his sword.

When the hell would Dumas run out?

Teaghan felt as if he were in some cheesy movie where the bad guys only ran out of bullets when it was dramatic, otherwise their guns kept firing forever. And Dumas was getting better at anticipating where Teaghan would dodge. One bullet ripped through Teaghan's pants, missing his leg. If he'd been wearing fitted clothing, that shot might have hit his shin.

{At least those stupid clothes serve some purpose. Incoming.}

A loud crack similar to a roll of thunder filled the air, and Dumas was thrown off his feet. Beyond him, his necromancer clutched his chest before falling to the ground unconscious. Teaghan could still hear the man's heart beating, but it was faint. He would worry about the necromancer later.

While Dumas was confused, Teaghan rushed him. He planted his foot on Dumas's chest, breaking the man's sternum, and then severed his head. Teaghan kicked the man's body a few times to vent his spleen before going to the fallen necromancer.

He asked Jeliyah, "What did you do?"

{A full-force Break. Without Shield in place, Dumas would have been chunks all over the parking lot. His necromancer, even as a Renfield, was still below my ability. The recoil from his Shield collapsing must have seized his heart. Is he okay?}

"He's alive. Without a vampire host to supply him, he's back to human healing. I'm sure he won't be thanking you later for letting him live." Teaghan slung the man over his shoulder and rushed back to Jeliyah.

She was still sitting on the ground behind the car when he came back. She hugged her arms while shivering.

"You a'right?"

"I've been better." She planted her hand on the ground and started to push to her feet, but lost strength and sat hard.

Teaghan hooked his free hand under her arm and pulled her to her feet. "Never had vampire blood before, huh?"

"It's severely frowned upon. And by frowned upon, I mean a rip is the least of my worries if anyone finds out."

"Get in the car."

She opened the door and collapsed onto the seat with a tired sigh. "If I had tried a Break that powerful without the help of your blood, I would have been comatose by now."

Teaghan nodded at the answer to his unspoken question of why she was in such bad shape. She'd had his blood and should be able to heal at a faster rate than normal. "So you're out of commission again?"

"No. If I needed to, I could still do a few more spells."

"You don't need to. Just sit there." Teaghan laid the necromancer he carried across the hood of the car and then pulled out his phone. His first call was to Fredrick at the reserve. After the man answered, Teaghan said, "Dumas is done. Bring my money, the cleanup crew, and an ambulance for his necromancer."

"The man is still alive?"

"Barely. Dumas made him a Renfield."

"A Renfield necromancer and you still managed to defeat him? Your new partner is more powerful than I thought."

"Yeah, she's something. Now hurry up." He ended the call and holstered the phone. "What would happen to you if those trustees of yours found out you drank my blood… without coercion?"

Jeliyah let her head fall back against the headrest with a sigh. "With or without doesn't matter. It's a rip either way. A big one. Punishment for such a big rip is time with one of the campus's resident vampires. How much time depends on the mood of the judge."

"Yeah, I heard 'bout resident vampires from someone who became one as punishment for something or other. Target practice for necro-trainees. He said those who run the campus handed him trainees that broke the rules and then egged him to take his frustrations out on them. Short of feeding, anything he did was kosher. Anything. And those left with him were forced to give an open invitation."

She gave a weak nod. "Make the punishment such that no one would ever even *think* of committing a crime. Tasting vampire blood willingly is one step away from becoming a willing Renfield, or that's how the trustees view it. A Renfield with a necromancer's abilities is dangerous to all other necromancers, which is why they get locked up if they're caught. To curtail the possibility, anyone found taking vampire blood will be used as the base for a new batch of necro-metal."

"Base? What's up with that?"

She laughed without humor. "It's a little poetic that necro-metal is made from blood, considering we use it to fight vampires. Platinums donate a few pints a year to create new batches of high-grade necro-metal. Costs a mint. Palladiums, like me, and those below donate our own blood to make the necro-metal we use, which is far more cost effective." She gestured one hand to the other. "This is me mixed with stainless steel and hematite."

"So they bleed offenders."

"Continually. Bleed them slowly enough that their blood replenishes, and they don't die. The blood is used for necromes that the campuses sell. If the offender is yellow gold and below, the necromes are given to trainees. Shortest bleeding term is five years. Longest recorded was sixteen, but that was for a longtime offender. Afterward, the necromancer isn't good for much, so they serve out the rest of their career until retirement—if they can even reach retirement—doing the jobs of a low level, which are maintaining the campus and teaching trainees."

"Why the fuck did you bite me? You want to stop being my partner bad enough to let the trustees bleed you?" Teaghan barely kept himself from yelling the words. There were people around. He didn't need someone overhearing this conversation.

"The only thing I could think of," she said in a tired voice. "Dumas was using his necromancer. That meant he might be a rogue himself or a Renfield. Either way, my help wouldn't have been worth dick without the boost from your blood to even the fight. And I needed my necromes to recognize you so I could help you fight without hitting you."

Teaghan started to ask her another question, but stopped when the sound of the ambulance siren reached his ears. It was about five miles away, if that much. That meant Fredrick—or whoever Fredrick had sent—and the cleanup crew wasn't far behind. He said to Jeliyah, "Play dead. We'll pick this up later."

"That's not going to be hard to do." She closed her eyes with a tired sigh.

He looked over her face to make sure no trace of his blood was on her. His lip had long since healed. He'd known this woman for two days, and he was already convinced she was crazy.

"I've been called worse," Jeliyah mumbled.

"Shut it. I told you to play dead."

"Yes, sir." Her tone was mock militant, which made Teaghan smile. He had something for her smart ass later. First, he had to deal with the wrap-up for this hunt and find them a new motel.

CHAPTER

FIVE

Jeliyah floated in and out of consciousness as Teaghan cleaned up after their latest escapade. She caught snippets of conversation and pieces of Teaghan's thoughts but didn't try to make sense of any of it.

Play dead... or at least play wiped out and recuperating. Which, at this point, she wasn't playing. Jeliyah couldn't move if she wanted. She hadn't lied. If not for Teaghan's blood, her little stunt with Break would have put her in a coma.

It scared her that she hadn't questioned her decision to take his blood. But the hum of necro-metal that belonged to Leslie—she'd recognized the man when Teaghan brought him back—had spurred her into action. She didn't know how far away Leslie had been from her when she felt it, but the power of his necromes had bumped against hers the moment she put on her rings.

She hadn't felt that when she came up against Leslie, the twins, and the other necromancer on that first hunt. She hadn't felt anything. If not for Dumas and Didios heading straight for Teaghan the moment he arrived to take out the rogue, she wouldn't have known the twins had necromancers with them.

True, no enforcer was supposed to hunt without a necromancer, but it wouldn't have been the first time an enforcer disobeyed that particular mandate.

Leslie's power boost, which put him on level with palladium and announced his presence—though not his exact location—to any necromancer in the vicinity, meant he'd tasted vampire blood.

Jeliyah had put her necromes in full deactivation two seconds after Teaghan decapitated Dumas. She didn't want anyone feeling her power the way she had felt Leslie's. She was in no hurry to be bled, despite what Teaghan might think. Neither was she in a hurry to die—and she was sure Dumas would have killed her after Teaghan—so she'd done the one thing that would keep them both alive.

The car door opening jarred her awake. She looked up at Teaghan, who loomed over her. Without a word, he scooped her into his arms and carried her to the new motel room. How long had she been sleeping that she had missed him checking in to a new motel?

The sun rising in the distance was her answer. They'd left the club around three in the morning. That meant it was past six. She'd gotten an hour-long nap, if that much. At least it felt as if she'd gotten more. She attributed that to Teaghan's blood in her system.

While she could walk on her own, it felt good letting him carry her. She enjoyed the ride as Teaghan climbed the stairs to the second-floor landing of the motel and headed for the room he'd gotten them.

Teaghan kicked the room door shut behind him and then laid her on the nearest bed. "At least this time you're not glowing. Let's not make a habit of this."

"I feel the same."

"Then again..." His gaze wandered to her breasts.

Images of Teaghan running his hands over her breasts and teasing her nipples entered her mind. She reared up and smacked him at the same time she brought her other arm up to guard her chest.

Teaghan didn't react except to grin. "You're flushed, necromancer. Your heart rate jumped too. My little idea get you all hot and bothered?"

She glared at him.

"No? How about this one?"

A mental picture of Teaghan yanking off her panties so he could run his tongue over her clit invaded her mind. The detail was so vivid, Jeliyah felt her pussy twitch in anticipation. Damn the man and this stupid mental connection. It might be one way, but she had access to his thoughts and now he wasn't trying to hide them. "You can't do that without an invitation."

"So invite me."

"Shouldn't you be going to sleep? The sun is up."

"Sun's got nothing to do with me." He moved closer, planting his hands on either side of her legs and leaning into her. "Invite me."

Jeliyah scooted back off the bed and away from him. Once on her feet, she said, "Don't get all cocky just because I took some of your blood, vampire. I told you that was a onetime thing and not to get ideas."

"Yeah, I heard you but—" he hopped the bed and crowded her against the wall "—here's the thing. You could have gotten the same results by asking me to open a vein. A simple prick to the finger for a few drops of blood would have sufficed. You kissed me, necromancer."

"It was a split-second decision. Back off." She clutched the necrome at her throat and said, "Shield."

Teaghan laughed as the shield expanded to include him. "Forget something important, did you? Your necromes recognize me now. I'm not a threat."

Shit!

She'd forgotten one of the major side effects of Recognize. Her necromes—and any others made from her blood—no longer worked against Teaghan. There was no way to deactivate Recognize either, just like someone couldn't rescind an invitation once given.

She shoved at his chest, but he kept leaning forward until his lips were close to hers.

He said, "Let's talk about that kiss."

"It was spur of the moment. It meant nothing."

"Care to test that theory?"

"You can't. I haven't invited you."

"Kissing is the one thing I don't need an invitation to do." He pushed his lips against hers as he forced her hands over her head and pressed his body closer.

Jeliyah couldn't turn from the kiss, though she tried. This wasn't fair. Vampires needed permission to enter a person's body. Why didn't that extend to kissing? And why was she giving in to his kiss?

Her body was betraying her. She didn't find Teaghan attractive in the least, with his wannabe lifestyle, yet she couldn't deny the heat making her nipples tighten and the low, needy moan that left her lips.

Teaghan pulled back and edged her feet apart with a few light kicks. He raised his knee between her legs until it pressed against the growing wet spot on her panties, then he smiled at her. "What were you saying about it meaning nothing?" He wiggled his knee side to side. "Is this nothing too?"

"Stop," Jeliyah rasped. A pitiful whimper escaped her lips when Teaghan filled her mind with graphic images of what he planned to do to her when she invited him.

When?

If. *If*, damn it. And not even that. She had no intention of inviting him.

The fiction books had gotten it partially right. It wasn't a living person's domicile to which a vampire needed an invitation. It was a living person's *body*. A vampire couldn't enter a human—that meant no biting, no sex, no penetration of any kind—without permission. Why kissing was exempt from that, Jeliyah didn't know and wanted to file a complaint with the person who had made the rules.

Teaghan bombarded her with his intentions, taking advantage of their one-way link and her inability to block his thoughts. Close to her ear, he said, "You're being a tease, Jeliyah. I smell your lust, and your juices are soaking through my jeans. Just invite me."

Her denial died on her lips when he cupped one of her breasts and kneaded. This shouldn't be allowed either, but it didn't qualify as penetration. Squirming to get out of his hold, only rubbed her panty-clad clit over his knee, which made her shiver with need.

He chuckled and licked her neck. "Invite me."

Jeliyah bit her lower lip to keep from speaking, from giving in. This was a vampire's nature. That pesky invitation clause hadn't stopped them from getting blood and sex over the centuries, because vampires were masters of seduction. She wouldn't be a notch on Teaghan's belt.

He sucked at her neck while thinking about lifting her dress to suck at her nipples in like manner. And then he moved to do it. He stopped kneading her breast long enough to lift the dress up, covering her head and baring her from the neck down. She couldn't see.

Teaghan unsnapped her bra. He imagined flicking one of her nipples with his tongue while rolling the other between his thumb and forefinger before doing both. Next came the image of him sucking her nipples in rapid succession, and then he did it. The show and act had Jeliyah panting with pleasure and the need for more.

Her mental coaching to stay strong crumbled as her body begged for release. "Teaghan."

He stilled his motions, and she got the picture of him smiling. He whispered in a low, seductive tone, "Say it, Jeliyah."

She swallowed. All her training and the warnings came to

mind. *Never give in to their allure. Vampires are dangerous.* She knew it all and yet she'd already ignored one necromancer edict—a major one. Jeliyah hadn't learned Recognize in the classroom. The book where she'd gotten it had named it a forbidden spell not to be taught or used—*ever.* Teaghan was immune to her necro-metal, but his only concern had been to seduce rather than hurt her.

This was stupid. She was riding an adrenaline high after being attacked twice and she felt grateful to Teaghan for saving her both times. That's all this was. She shouldn't compound the issue and make her situation worse.

"I invite you," she whispered.

Teaghan pulled her dress off and deposited her on the bed with a speed that made her gasp. He made good on his earlier mental threat of yanking off her panties but didn't dive between her legs as he'd shown he would. Instead, he held her legs open at the knees and lowered himself so his face was close to her exposed pussy.

"Very pretty." His breath tickled her hot, slick flesh.

He opened his mouth wide, and she gasped, twitching her legs and jutting toward his mouth. Teaghan grinned at her. "I haven't done anything yet, necromancer. Eager?"

She wanted to kick him. "Let go. I changed my mind."

"You know invitations don't work like that." He laid a kiss on her clit, which made Jeliyah yelp with need. "And your mind might be changed, but the rest of you is begging me to continue. This part, for instance."

He spread her legs more and then licked around the edge of her pussy entrance. Her hips rocked as she huffed in reaction to that simple contact. Something so small had her close to the edge.

She covered her face, trying to block the reality of what she was doing even as she enjoyed the way Teaghan's tongue danced between her entrance and her clit. A sharp cry of pleasure left her when he puckered his lips over her nub and sucked—a quick pull before letting go with a loud pop.

Her panting filled the room before she realized the sound was coming from her. Teaghan returned and sucked at her clit again. This time longer, harder. He drew on her nub while flicking his tongue over the hood.

She tried to close her legs against the delicious sensation, but Teaghan held her open with ease. He slid his hands to her thighs and kneaded as he continued, sending bolts of delight through her body from her clit.

The orgasm that claimed Jeliyah arched her back almost in half as she screamed her release. The person in the room next door pounded on the wall several times, but Jeliyah didn't quiet until Teaghan lifted his mouth. She sagged, panting and whimpering. The twitching of her over-sensitized clit sent tingles down the insides of her thighs.

The sound of a zipper rasping open preceded Teaghan crawling over Jeliyah so he could smile down at her. "Foreplay time is over. Now for the real fun." His smile grew larger when his canines started elongating.

Jeliyah's heart rate sped up. What had she done? She braced her hands on Teaghan's chest, tangling in his gold chains, but knew that wouldn't hold him back. Not now. Not after inviting him. "I didn't say you could feed on me." It was a pitiful attempt to stop the inevitable, and she knew it.

Teaghan captured her wrists and moved her hands above her head again. "You gave an open invitation, Jeliyah. You're a necromancer and know better than to simply invite a vampire without ground rules." He lowered his head. "Too late now."

He rested his fangs on her neck but didn't bite her. What was he waiting for? She was at his mercy through her own stupidity. His fangs grazed her skin as he moved his head back and forth. He was toying with her. Jeliyah squeezed her eyes shut, preparing for the pain she knew was coming.

A babbling brook complete with tweeting birds and chirping

insects played through Teaghan's mind. He said in a low voice, "I'm not a punishment, Jeliyah. This isn't the campus."

"I know where I am," she snapped, yanking on her hands to get them free.

Teaghan's hold remained firm. "Then you know I'm not trying to hurt you." He slipped one hand down her side and under her, positioning it at her lower back. After splaying his fingers, he urged her up so her pussy nudged the tip of his dick. "There's no time limit. No one telling me to make you sorry for being bad."

A little shimmy eased his dick past her pussy lips. Teaghan moved his lower body in a scooping motion that seated his hard erection inside her to the base. Jeliyah keened low in her throat and squirmed beneath him at how right he felt.

"No one knows what you've done but me. It's going to stay that way so I can take full advantage of the situation. Agreed?" He punctuated his question by grinding against her, stirring her inside.

Jeliyah nodded quickly as she looped her legs around his back.

"Good. That's settled." Teaghan's thoughts shifted from the babbling brook to a raging waterfall that beat the rocks on the shore below. He shifted back and then returned, sliding in and out of her. Each thrust was faster than the last until Teaghan pounded into her with the force of the waterfall he showed her.

She barely registered the feel of his fangs as he bit her neck and fed. He didn't take more than a few sips before kissing his way down to one of her breasts.

He circled her nipple with the tip of his tongue. "Love your breasts." He released her wrists and then cupped the twin mounds and wiggled his fingers, making her breasts jiggle. That got a pleased laugh from him as he watched.

Jeliyah couldn't help joining him since it felt a little funny.

Before he could go back to toying her breasts with his tongue, if that was his plan, Jeliyah grabbed his gold chains and yanked them off. He didn't stop her. She tossed them aside. "Better."

"I'd rather have you around my neck, anyway." He reared back and then positioned her legs so they hung over his shoulders. Holding her steady as he leaned forward once more, he continued treating her pussy to the full length of his dick in quick, even strokes. "Flexible. I like that."

Jeliyah had no answer to give since she was too busy moaning loud enough to have their neighbor banging on the wall again. She crossed her ankles behind Teaghan's neck since the position didn't allow her to hug him.

He felt so right and filled every part of her, but she wanted more. So much more. She hadn't felt anything this good in years. Many long years, so the second orgasm creeping over her so soon after the first didn't surprise her in the least. She tried to hold it back, to hold out so she could enjoy Teaghan more.

The man didn't make it easy. He stuffed his dick deep and stirred his hips against hers, his tip teasing her core and triggering her release. She bucked beneath him, calling his name.

Teaghan grinned and resumed thrusting, riding her through the orgasm. "We're not done yet, necromancer. Not by a long shot." He paused so he could flip her onto her stomach and pull her to her knees.

The man had skills, since he did all that without his dick leaving her pussy. Or maybe it had, but he moved so swiftly that it felt as if it hadn't. With one hand palming one of her breasts and the other rubbing her clit, he resumed pounding into her.

Jeliyah balled the bedding in her fists, but that didn't help anchor her to reality. Teaghan swept her along at his pace, as he'd been doing since she met him. Her body craved his attention, and she cried out, "Please. Oh please."

"Right here, Jeliyah. All you could want. Just tell me how much." Teaghan rolled her clit between two fingers.

Her arms collapsed beneath her. She whimpered, unsure if it was a sound meant to tell him to stop or give her more. Nothing made sense except the pleasure.

Fine shivers shook her and her muscles tensed as another orgasm grabbed hold of her. This one froze her movements, leaving her with only the ability to shudder and pant.

Teaghan grunted and braced his hands on her waist as he came with her, spilling himself inside her depths. He pulled free once he was spent. "Damn good."

Jeliyah sagged onto the bed with her face buried in the sheets to cover her shame. It didn't help. The afterglow didn't cover up everything she'd done wrong—sharing blood, an open invitation, and sex with a vampire. How had her life gone so totally out of control in such a short amount of time?

Of her three transgressions, sharing blood was the worst. She was one step away from being a Renfield.

"Chill." Teaghan lay down beside her and pulled her against his side so her head rested on his shoulder. "You're not a Renfield. It takes more than sharing a little blood for that to happen."

She touched her head and then gasped softly. "I forgot you can hear my thoughts now."

"Part of sharing blood. Enough with the self-recrimination. You got laid, not committed treason."

"It might as well be treason." Jeliyah's memory flashed to the tour of the necro-metal factory all trainees had to take. It was a scare tactic more than an educational visit. The trainers had made sure their charges saw a punished necromancer being bled. A warning.

The man had been a palladium level who had gotten too close to the vampires he worked with. A night of sex and blood sharing had led to him to being strapped to a hospital bed with one IV in one arm draining blood while another IV in his other arm supplied nutrients for sustained life.

"Holy fucking shit," Teaghan rasped as he pulled back and looked at her. "How old were you when you saw that?"

"Fourteen. I had nightmares for weeks after. Most of us did."

"Vampires don't dream, but that shit's going to give me

nightmares. And you all call us monsters. Who does that to another human being?"

"Necromancers. We're not human. Not completely." She laughed without humor. "An extra letter in our blood type and our chromosomes that makes it easy for the government to find us, but that science cannot explain. The same magic that animates you makes us, though not many will admit to it. Once a trainee enters the campus, they're government property until retirement."

Teaghan settled down beside her and cupped the back of her head, kneading in a soft, soothing manner. "After the shit you just showed me, I'm almost afraid to ask about retirement."

"None of your previous partners told you?"

"We didn't talk. We didn't room together either. It's code for something. What?"

"Freedom." Jeliyah relaxed as the goal of retirement—assuming she could keep her transgression a secret until then—entered her mind. "The campus takes charge of necromancer potentials at age twelve. That care isn't free. Every single thing has a price tag on it, from the bandages to the food we eat. They give each child a limitless credit card. We're allowed to buy whatever we want." She laughed without humor. "It's a trap, of course. We're expected to pay back every cent after we graduate. Retirement is the debt paid in full. After that, a necromancer can seek gainful employment away from the campus, usually with a platinum who has a team in place guarding some rich person."

"So that's the big deal. But it's not real freedom. If it was, you would stop being a necromancer."

"Well, yeah. There is that. Once a necromancer, always a necromancer. We're too rare. If a retiree doesn't find a job fast enough, the trustees place them somewhere. The only way out of this gig is death."

"At least I can quit being an enforcer when I feel like it. You necromancers are paid slaves."

She didn't like the direction of the conversation. Revealing so much about necromancer life to an outsider grated against her sense of responsibility. "Why are you an enforcer? You looked like you were having more fun at the club. You make a ton of money each night. Maybe not as much as a rogue hunt, but you wouldn't be starving."

"I like killing people. I became a vampire on the battlefield. After I got out from under my sire, I kept at it. Some legal killings. Some not. Got on the bad side of some vampire hunters before I became a bounty hunter." He shrugged. "Pretending to be human costs, and I got paid to kill people. It was a win-win. The cost of living has gone up since the outing, but then, so have the bounties."

"Even if you're called enforcers now."

He snorted. "Humans and their fucking sugarcoating."

"It's all about spinning it to the public. The head families and the trustees want everyone to think the world is still the same, even though vampires are no longer fiction."

"Hell, at least we didn't get outed in Bram Stoker's time. No coexisting back then. He got damn close with that book of his. The families almost sent a hunter after his head and the heads of the entire Van Helsing clan who acted as his source."

"The necromancers' guild of the time got to them first. No one has heard from the Van Helsings since. One of the campus books I read hinted that the whole family—most of them platinum level—ended up in the necro-metal vats. Another said they were just killed outright. Still another said the family was delivered to the vampires to deal with. Whatever the true story, they didn't survive that book being published."

"Snitches don't get stitches in our world. They get dead." His hand tangled in her hair and pulled so she met his gaze. "Your secret is safe, Jeliyah."

"Thanks. Though how pathetic am I that I do something like this after two days in the field?"

"Based on the way you were begging for more, I would say you were due for a good lay."

"You're not wrong." She rolled out of his hold and sat up. The date of the last time she'd had sex eluded her. It was well before she graduated from the campus and joined Hirsch's precinct.

The trustees encouraged trainees to seek intimacy with each other. The coed sleeping arrangements all but guaranteed it. Necromancers gave birth to necromancers. The trustees wanted babies, recruits they could train from the cradle, which meant they didn't care about teen pregnancy.

Jeliyah's prospective partners dried up after she found out she couldn't get pregnant and her closest friend—the girl she thought was her closest friend—spilled the news to everyone else. The girl had done it to get the boy who had been interested in Jeliyah. After the news spread and the trainers verified it, Jeliyah had gotten her own room and all the solo training time she could wish for, even if she hadn't wanted it.

That inability to get pregnant was also why she was palladium level and not platinum, as she should be. The trainers at the campus felt her infertility outweighed her skills. So Teaghan was right to think she was too powerful to be out in the field with him, because she was. But her defect meant out in the field was where she had to be.

She heard Teaghan shift behind her. He probably made noise so as not to startle her, since the man was normally quiet, like all vampires. She stood before he could touch her. She needed a shower. The time alone would clear her thoughts and help her figure out the future.

She didn't say anything as she walked to the bathroom and closed the door behind her. The hot spray of the shower water had just started soothing her frayed nerves when the curtain opened. Teaghan stood naked and staring at her. Without a word, she stepped back in the tub, giving him room to enter.

He stepped into the spray of water, facing her. Water cascaded over his shoulders and down his chest. A chest that sported a diagonal, sunken scar that spanned from his left shoulder to his right side.

Jeliyah hesitantly touched the scar. She whispered, "What happened?" He could only have gotten the wound in life because vampires healed everything without a trace.

"You're right. This is what killed me. A battle-axe to the chest. Hurt like hell. I thought I was dead until my sire showed up." He gave her a rueful smile. "Just think. A few more minutes and I wouldn't be standing here now to annoy you."

"You don't annoy me."

"Don't I?"

She looked away from the scar to the rest of him. Tight abs, though not defined, a slim waist and strong legs. This man had been a warrior when he was alive, not some pampered lord or farmhand. A body like this one had been honed in war.

She trailed her fingers down over his stomach, hovering above his erection. Her pussy twitched in response. "You should be everything I hate, but I don't." She lifted her gaze to his. "Why don't I?"

"You're asking the wrong man, sweetness." He walked forward a few steps until her back pressed against the cold tile wall.

He captured her mouth with his in a hot kiss that banished the chill of being away from the shower water. Jeliyah wrapped her arms around his neck, welcoming his passion because it also chased away her other thoughts.

Teaghan lifted her high against the wall with his hands cupping her thighs and entered her pussy in a swift forward thrust. His and Jeliyah's cries of pleasure echoed off the walls. She huffed at the force of Teaghan's dick driving to her depths.

The first time wasn't a fluke. All the urgency and satisfaction from before returned in cascades. She grabbed Teaghan's head and kissed him hard, shoving her tongue into his mouth, greedy to taste him. He took the kiss and responded with a hunger of his own.

Everything else be damned. The trustees could kiss her ass. Teaghan felt too good to be wrong.

"That's the way, Jeliyah. Forget them and focus on me." He moved faster.

"Teaghan. Teaghan." She cried his name over and over. The rest of her life spanned before her to regret this, but for now she only cared about her pleasure and the man giving it to her.

Her orgasm washed through her, clearing everything away except for a sense of utter fulfillment. She buried her face against Teaghan's neck and tears of joy mixed with the shower water.

She clutched his shoulders, digging her nails into his skin, and squeezed him tight with her thighs and inner muscles. He grunted and slowed his pace as he came. His final stroke left him nestled deep and snug. She didn't want to let him go, to let go of the idea that everything would be all right.

"Just us, necromancer. Just us." Teaghan imparted those words as he hugged her waist.

She nodded, but didn't loosen her hold. When the adrenaline wore off, when she got some rest, when the world returned to normal, she would see there was nothing to be worried about. Sex left no telltale signs. So long as she and Teaghan kept their mouths shut, no one would ever know she wasn't a model necromancer.

CHAPTER
SIX

Jeliyah took another bite of her burrito, ignoring the way Teaghan covered his nose and breathed through his mouth. His exaggerated reaction to her choice of food only made her want to get another.

"Don't even think about it, necromancer," he snapped.

"I'm downwind."

"That stuff is still foul. How can you eat it?"

"Well, I'm sorry I'm not on a liquid diet like some people. Regular food has smells. Get over it."

"Regular food smells better. That is garbage wrapped in a fried flour tortilla. Month old, sitting in the summer sun, garbage." He tightened his hand over his nose.

She didn't take pity on him. The burrito might not smell good, but it tasted fantastic. Besides, this Mexican restaurant was the only place on the way to the club—something Teaghan had insisted on since they got a late start thanks to him wanting a quickie.

"Don't put that all on me, necromancer. I didn't exactly hear you complaining."

Jeliyah didn't acknowledge his words and tried hard to think of something else so the memories of how they had spent the early evening, after a day of sleeping in each other's arms, wouldn't get her aroused. Invitation or not, they couldn't keep having sex. Each time upped the chances of someone finding out their relationship had gone past a simple partnership.

That might be paranoid, but she would rather be paranoid than strapped to a hospital bed and bled.

"You done?"

She crumpled the food wrapper into a tight ball and walked her trash to the waste bin. "Done."

"Let's go then." Teaghan stalked back to the car. He cursed under his breath once he got to the driver's side. "Look at this shit."

"Are you going to bitch about your car each time you get in to drive?" Jeliyah opened the passenger door and slid onto her seat. She'd gotten better at getting in and out. There was a trick to it. Once she had figured that out, it became less of a struggle.

Teaghan hopped over the door. She hadn't seen him open it yet. He snapped, "If the fucker wasn't already dead, I would strap him to my bumper and drag him down the highway doing ninety." He peeled out of the parking lot and headed for the club.

"Why did he do it?"

"Shoot up my car? Because he was an evil fucker. Why else?"

"Would you forget about your damn car for five seconds? You have enough money after turning in his head—even after giving me half—to get it fixed or junk it and get a new one. I'm talking about why Dumas went rogue. Enforcers have infighting, I get that. What I don't get is going kill-all-humans after a missed hunt. What set him off?"

"Fuck all if I know. The twins were crazy long before they went rogue. They tortured small animals when they were kids, I'm sure. It shouldn't have taken them that long to kill that rogue from our first hunt. They were probably playing with him."

"So you show up, steal the toy prize, and they suddenly decide to kill one necromancer and then try to kill me? That makes no sense."

"I told you already. Sense and the twins weren't friends. They're dead. You aren't. Leave it at that, necromancer."

Jeliyah dropped the subject, but it still bothered her.

"What should be bothering you is that outfit."

"There's nothing wrong with my outfit." Jeans and a cotton shirt might be a little too casual for the club, but it was all she had. She wasn't wearing that micro-mini dress again. First, it was too short. Second, it smelled like sex and sweat. Third, the people at the club had already seen her in it once.

"Never took you for the superficial type."

"Stop doing that, damn it. Someone's going to catch on that we've shared blood if you keep responding to me and I haven't said anything."

Spotting blood partners—what people called a human and a vampire who had shared blood—was easy when someone knew the signs. The biggest tip-off was the one-sided conversations. It was like someone talking on a cellphone, except the conversation partner was right there.

"My bad. That doesn't change the travesty of what you're wearing. Don't worry though. One of the girls should have another outfit for you."

"I don't need a different outfit. This one is fine." She didn't relish the thought of yet another micro-mini or any of the other outfits Nessa had trotted out the night before.

"No, it's not and we're doing some shopping after this is over. You're not going to keep embarrassing me each night."

"So let me stay at the motel."

"No."

"I don't want to waste money on clothes I don't want."

"So I'll waste my money. Give in, necromancer. The club is going to happen along with your wardrobe change. Your body is on. Show it off. You won't have to pay for your drinks or food the whole night."

"I don't need someone else to pay my way."

"Oh? I thought you were saving for retirement."

"A few drinks and a snack aren't going to set back my retirement plans that much."

"Every little bit helps."

"No." She refused and would keep refusing. She was moving at Teaghan's pace again. It annoyed her how easily he led her, as though she couldn't think for herself when she'd been doing it for a while now. They should be in separate motel rooms and only mingling when on a hunt. He had his life, and she had hers.

"Don't kid yourself, necromancer. You have no life."

"I said stop it!"

"Sorry. Damn."

She hated someone having free access to her thoughts without her having a say in what they heard and what they saw. Teaghan had control of it. She'd seen evidence of that already. She didn't hear every thought he had, while some came through as though she'd thought them herself.

The connection would wear off soon. She hoped. She hadn't taken that much of his blood and he'd only fed on her that once. The invitation might be permanent, but the shared thoughts had a time limit.

She rubbed her fingers over her necklace. Teaghan had told her to keep it on tonight. He also told her to stash her pouch of necromes in the car glove box. Neither of them wanted a repeat of last night.

The club parking lot was packed, and the door had a line curved around the building when they arrived. The gruesome battle of the night before hadn't hurt the club's popularity in the least. True, most of the guests had been gone when Jeliyah was attacked, but she figured word would have spread.

The only thing spreading in that club were the legs of the

women who flocked Teaghan the second he stepped foot on the premises.

{*No need to be jealous, necromancer.*} Teaghan's deep voice rumbled through her mind.

{*Shut it. No telepathy either,*} she snapped.

He pointed Nessa in Jeliyah's direction.

The blonde asked in annoyance, "Again?"

Jeliyah wanted to smack the woman. What did Nessa have to be pissed about? Jeliyah didn't want to borrow her clothes.

Teaghan smacked the woman's ass, which made her giggle. "Go to it. I've got work to do."

Rather than try to fight it like the night before, Jeliyah followed the woman.

Jeliyah vetoed anything that showed her ass. That left her with a close-knit fishnet, ankle-length dress. Strategically placed horizontal strips at her chest and waist made it the best option. It came with a matching bra and panties. Nessa tried to get Jeliyah into the thong instead of the panties, but Jeliyah threatened to get her gun and shoot the woman. Panties it was.

Jeliyah wanted a more substantial outfit. She was wearing less than the night before and hadn't even known that was possible. Given the wardrobe options and her need for clothing that didn't push her comfort boundaries, Jeliyah knew she would be shopping with Teaghan tomorrow after all.

His smug laughter filled her head. She gave him the mental equivalent of the finger. The shopping trip was self-preservation. She didn't want to see what Nessa would put her in tomorrow if the woman was forced to dress her again.

The dress got Jeliyah all the attention Teaghan said it would. Men fell over themselves all night to buy her drinks—strong drinks —and food. They were more willing to get her drinks than food, but gave in when she resorted to batting her eyelashes and asking in a cutesy voice.

It wasn't Jeliyah's usual style to flirt, but that didn't mean she didn't know how to do it and when. Besides, the food at the club was worth it. Teaghan hadn't mentioned that when stopping to get her burrito. Then again, he was a vampire. He wouldn't have known the club's food was good.

Between drinks, the men convinced Jeliyah to dance. She figured she owed them that much since they wouldn't get anything else out of her, no matter how many drinks they bought. Necromancer metabolism—she couldn't get drunk. The same thing made poison ineffectual as well.

Correction—a necromancer could get drunk, but it took a rare, very expensive type of alcohol to do it. She doubted the club had it. Even if they did, her admirers didn't have pockets deep enough to afford a capful, let alone the many glasses needed to get her tipsy.

The night wore on and Jeliyah's admirers left one by one as they realized she wouldn't sound the easy-girl mating call of *I'm so drunk* any time soon. She would have felt bad for them if they hadn't been planning to take advantage of her while she was inebriated.

"Poor idiots don't know a necromancer when they see one," said a man close to Jeliyah's shoulder.

She glanced back at him but knew already he was a vampire. That didn't surprise her. The club had a substantial vampire population. What surprised her was him speaking to her. The other vampires had kept their distance all night.

She said, "Most humans don't. We're not easy to spot like vampires." She tapped her lip to indicate his fangs. They got longer when a vampire was preparing to feed, but the non-feeding fangs were still longer than a normal human's canines.

"So you acknowledge necromancers are not human."

"We're mortal. Human is debatable."

"How refreshing to hear you say that." He gestured to the empty seat at the bar beside her. "May I join you?"

"If you want."

He leaned his back against the edge of the bar and looked over the crush of dancers. "Who are you hunting?"

"I'm not."

"Is that so? I saw you here last night and heard about the rogue kill that happened afterward. I thought you might be hunting someone."

"Nope. Just here to have fun. The rogue wasn't a club patron. He came here for me."

"I see. Sounds like a dangerous life."

She shrugged, not that concerned. She'd been raised as a necromancer. The lesson of danger existing around every corner so long as vampires were allowed to walk amongst humans as equals had been drilled into her from her first days on the campus. The vampires didn't like the necromancers any more than the necromancers liked vampires—natural enemies forced to tolerate each other to keep the tenuous peace.

She asked, "So, where's your necromancer tonight?"

The man laughed, showing fangs. "I should have known you would recognize me as an enforcer without your necrome being active." He offered his hand. "I'm Ephraim."

She shook his hand briefly, not wanting to touch him but not wanting to be rude either. At least her aversion to vampires was still intact. Teaghan must be the exception.

She said, "It took me a moment to sense your marker, but I doubt a normal vampire who suspected me of being a necromancer would open the conversation asking about hunts. The vampire population is as much in denial about rogues as the humans."

"Very true. Very true. My partner opted for a movie. I got bored and decided to try out this club. Several have recommended it to me. They are right. The vampire DJ is good at his job."

She made a noncommittal sound, not willing to admit Teaghan was good, not aloud. Sex or not, his wannabe lifestyle still grated on her nerves.

"And where is your partner? After your run-in last night, I doubt he would send you out alone."

She gestured to the DJ booth where Teaghan performed his job while surrounded by women. "He's moonlighting. And you're right. He wouldn't leave me alone, and that's why I'm here."

"Ah. From the edge in your voice, I take you aren't fond of clubs."

"Too loud. Too crowded. I would rather be at home, but I lost the argument."

"If your home is far from here, it would explain his reluctance to leave you there. He wouldn't be able to render you aid if you were attacked again."

Jeliyah's skin prickled as a sense of warning swept through her. Her paranoia might be flaring up, but she wouldn't ignore the sensation, not after having one enforcer attack her. The way Ephraim phrased his statement made her think he might be trying to find out where she and Teaghan were staying. Again, moving motels after every hunt proved to be a sound strategy.

She said in a measured tone, while trying not to sound measured, "He just likes to show off how popular he is. I think he wants to make nice with me, which is cute and all—especially for someone his age—but he's a means to an end. I'm not looking for friends."

Ephraim chuckled as he nodded. "A necromancer through and through. All about retirement. I have to stop my partner from accepting hunts for us at times. The man doesn't want to give me time to rest."

"Funny that there are so many hunts in the last few months. Add two enforcers going rogue and a casual observer might think something was going on in the vampire nation. What do you think?"

It was his turn to be guarded. Jeliyah wouldn't have noticed the way he relaxed more, as though forcing himself to appear relaxed when he really wasn't, if she hadn't been watching him out of the corner of her eye while pretending not to be watching him. He knew something.

Ephraim said, "The head family has made no statements to indicate something is amiss."

"Like they would."

"True."

Jeliyah wanted to get away from the man. She sent a mental cry of help to Teaghan to get her away from Ephraim without looking as if she was running. Her internal alarm sounded loud and clear. Everything about Ephraim put her on edge, and she didn't have centuries of practice, like him, to pretend she wasn't on edge. Not for long.

The bartender tapped her shoulder. She spun and faced him. "Yes?"

"Teag's calling you." He pointed at the DJ booth.

Jeliyah looked in Teaghan's direction. He was waving her over with one hand in the air. It almost looked as if he was dancing. She didn't care. She needed the out. To Ephraim, she said, "I have to see what he wants."

"Of course. Don't let me keep you."

She kept her pace sedate as she walked to the DJ booth. Without looking over her shoulder to confirm, she knew Ephraim was watching her and not because of her outfit. If she did anything to indicate she saw him as a threat, he would attack her. She felt that intention loud and clear.

What the hell had she done to get on the enforcer hit list? Her gaze went to Teaghan. Maybe it was him. Had he put a target on his back and she was catching shit by association? Maybe taking the twins' hunt and forcing them to go rogue had broken some enforcer-brotherhood code, and now the others were hazing him. Whatever the case, Jeliyah didn't appreciate being caught in the middle.

She squeezed into the booth, elbowing aside a few of the girls, who glared at her. They didn't say anything, which was good because Jeliyah would have had some things to say right back.

Teaghan pulled her close and leaned into her. He didn't whisper in her ear, though. His words sounded in her head. {*Can you activate your necrome in silent mode or something?*}

{*Why?*}

{*I'm thinking he's not the only enforcer in here. I need to know what I'm up against.*}

{*You're flying blind. If I activate this necrome, every vampire in the club will know it.*}

He nodded and released her to go back to his music.

Jeliyah moved to the back wall of the booth. A quick glance at the bar showed Ephraim still there and still looking her way. She decided to act as if Teaghan had scolded her. Crossing her arms over her chest, she fixed a pout on her face.

It wasn't hard acting upset. She was. But her upset was tinged with apprehension and a small amount of fear. They were going to be attacked again.

CHAPTER

SEVEN

Teaghan was monitoring three vampires while acting as if he were absorbed in the music. The first had been Ephraim. He'd gotten the man's name from Jeliyah's mind since Teaghan didn't know him. It had pissed off Teaghan when a vampire came sniffing after Jeliyah once the humans gave up.

Her outfit was doing too damn good a job. He'd wanted to loosen her up so it would be that much easier to get her in bed again once they returned to the hotel, not help her find another sex partner. He figured they were in for another argument before he convinced her to give in to what she really wanted—him.

With one confirmed and two other possible enforcers stalking them, an argument about sex was the least of his worries. Jeliyah's question about the twins' motivation in going rogue entered his mind. Blowing it off earlier might not have been his wisest move.

He didn't know what this was, though. Enforcers didn't attack other enforcers, not unless they had gone rogue. And there was no way someone had tagged Teaghan as a rogue. If they had, the enforcers wouldn't sit around letting him spin tunes all night. Humans or not, they would attack him to keep him from rabbiting.

The head family liked enforcers to do rogue takedowns without witnesses, but they preferred the rogue to be killed as quickly as possible. So Teaghan didn't have rogue status. What he had was just as annoying, though.

He agreed with Jeliyah's assessment about Ephraim's interest in the motel and how close it was to the club. It was across town on purpose. Teaghan kept home and play well away from each other. If a rogue found Teaghan's motel, he wanted to make sure the fight didn't endanger his favorite pastime.

"Need a drink, Teaghan?"

The redhead who spoke pulled Teaghan out of his thoughts. His gaze went to her neck. "Yeah, I do." If a fight was coming, he needed to be fed.

The girl giggled and cooed as he slipped his arm around her waist and pulled her close. She tilted her head back, pressing her breasts against his chest and rubbing her thigh against his hip. Her open invitation annoyed him, but that didn't mean he wouldn't take the drink she offered.

He bit her and fed quick, taking two pints. His giggling donor moaned with passion. She mistook vertigo for pleasure. Not his problem. He released her, ignoring her stumbling movements, and grabbed another girl to feed him.

Anyone who knew him would notice his out-of-character actions. Teaghan didn't indulge. He sipped at the donors supplied to him, giving each enough attention so they would volunteer again the next time he showed up. A few sips spread out over five-to-seven girls equaled a meal for him.

That's all the girls were—dinner. Before Jeliyah came into his life, he would have singled out one girl for a quickie in the back office once the club closed to feed his other hunger. A player's lifestyle. One he enjoyed. Jeliyah—his abrasive little necromancer —compelled his full attention, whether she wanted it or not. He planned to do all in his power to keep her safe.

He released the second girl, and a third rushed forward to take her place, baring her neck and her breasts in one movement. Not long ago, such a display would have had Teaghan pushing her up against the table to fuck her while he continued mixing music. Now, his dick didn't so much as twitch.

Yup, his necromancer had done a number on him. He was glad he had practice blocking his thoughts or else she would pick that fact from his mind. He planned to have her take responsibility for impeding on his lifestyle as soon as he was sure they wouldn't be killed.

"Done," he said to the girl.

She pouted and stroked his side, running a single finger along the top of his pants. "Come on, Teag. Me too. Please," she purred.

A quick glance around the booth showed the remaining three girls were eagerly awaiting their turns and would be just as demanding as the one in front of him.

{Just do it, vampire, before she makes a scene.} Jeliyah's annoyed tone let him know he would pay for his feedings later.

He bit the girl in front of him, feeding a little and then letting her go. He was close to full. Too much blood and he would be too drunk to fight, making him sluggish and uncoordinated.

The last three girls got their nip-and-sucks out of the way and left Teaghan in peace. He went back to watching the three vampires, waiting for them to do something he could claim was threatening so he could take them out.

They were watching him the way he watched them. He had no doubt they were all aware of the situation as it stood. Teaghan had called his necromancer close to him and fed enough to ensure he'd be at the top of his game if a fight broke out. Jeliyah's rings might be in the car, but she had her necklace, and he'd strapped his sword to his back as well and had her gun tucked in his calf harness under his jeans.

Since Lee trusted him, Teaghan didn't have to go through the normal weapon searches as the other club patrons. Teaghan hoped tonight wouldn't change that. He would hate to stop working with Lee over the issue of protecting himself.

Teaghan cued up a song with lyrics that sent a clear message to the other enforcers—*your move.*

The two vampires Teaghan suspected were enforcers left the club. Ephraim toasted Teaghan with Jeliyah's discarded drink and then followed them.

Teaghan didn't know what was happening. After this, he planned to find out. He glanced over his shoulder at Jeliyah.

She said, *{I know. We're moving motels again.}*

{Not just motels. We're getting the fuck out of town. I'm putting some distance between us and them so we can figure this shit out.}

{Sounds like a plan.}

Teaghan would have to break the bad news to Lee about not being able to do the rest of the week. He planned to say a hunt came up. Lee wouldn't whine as much with that excuse.

The rest of the night passed with only the normal level of club excitement. The enforcers didn't return, but Teaghan wasn't stupid enough to think they had left.

At the end of the night, he offered the bogus hunt excuse to Lee before hustling Jeliyah out of the club and to the car. He'd pulled his earplugs the second the music stopped so he could hear anything and everything. No way was he repeating last night and letting some asshole get the drop on him.

Jeliyah's nervous fear filled his thoughts, though she tried to put up a brave façade. She relaxed once they were in the car and on the highway, headed back to the motel. She asked, "What's going on?"

"I'm finding out now." Teaghan pulled his phone, hit the speed dial for Fredrick and then laid the phone on the dash. The ringing filtered through the car speakers.

"Hello, Teaghan. I thought you might be calling me soon."

Teaghan snapped, "What the hell is this, Fredrick? I've got three enforcers sniffing after my ass."

Fredrick laughed. "You're not as sharp as I thought if you only spotted three, Teaghan."

He gritted his teeth. That wasn't what he wanted to hear. He glanced in the rearview mirror. The highway was the perfect place for a tail to hide. There was no way to spot a car following when they were all going in the same direction. Teaghan took the next exit, deciding to use the city roads instead.

He said, "Why are you after me, Fredrick?"

"I couldn't care less about you. I'm following orders. The one giving the orders was more than a little put out when you killed that rogue."

Teaghan and Jeliyah exchanged a glance.

Fredrick said, "I made sure Hirsch chose someone who would pique your interest enough to blow off the hunt in favor of getting in her pants. I underestimated your greed."

"Tell me this isn't some fucked-up revenge because Dipshit and Dumbass didn't get to take out the rogue."

"No, this is punishment for killing a rogue who shouldn't have been touched. Didios and Dumas already paid the price for their failure to keep him alive long enough to make a very important meeting. Thank you for that, by the way. However, now it's your turn."

Teaghan knew it. A coup was about to happen. He didn't know the players and didn't care. So long as the bills got paid, the person in power didn't matter. From one leader to the next, nothing ever changed.

He said, "Fine. You want me. I get that. Leave the necromancer out of it. No one would miss me, but take her out and you'll have the trustees gunning for you and your boss."

"You're right. The trustees would be quite upset if we killed the necromancer, and that wasn't my intention. The others wanted to have some fun with her before handing her over, but that was all."

Jeliyah gripped the door handle, and her eyes widened.

Teaghan said, "The trustees won't overlook you molesting one of their own."

"That's where you're wrong. They've given us permission to do with her as we please, so long we return her to them intact."

Jeliyah yelled, "They would never do that."

Fredrick chuckled. "Well, hello, Jeliyah. Ephraim tells me you smell of vampire seed and blood. Recent seed. Old blood. I had thought you would hold out against Teaghan much longer, given your initial reaction to him. Either I overestimated you or underestimated him." He made the vocal equivalent of a shrug. "Doesn't matter since I felt the need to pass on the news of your little indiscretion to Hirsch, who then relayed it to the trustees. They are very displeased that a palladium level such as yourself would give a vampire permission to invade her body. That displeasure graduated to anger when I informed them of the blood sharing as well."

Oh please, no. No. No.

Teaghan grabbed Jeliyah's hand in a firm grip to anchor her to the here and now. She clutched at him and stared at his profile. Tears rimmed her eyes. He knew she was holding it together by a thin thread of will. Images of the bleeding chamber raced through her mind. She was imagining herself in the place of the person she'd seen when she was young.

He said, {*I've got you, Jeliyah. Nothing's going to happen.*}

Fredrick said, "Stop the car and give up. Make this easier for all of us."

"Denied." Teaghan released Jeliyah's hand so he could snatch the phone off the dash and hit the end button.

Jeliyah asked, "What do we do? They want you dead and me—" Her words choked to a halt and she pulled in a shuddering breath. A single tear slipped down her cheek.

He retrieved her hand and squeezed it. "Easy there, necromancer. Don't fall apart on me now."

"Why? All you did was kill a rogue."

"That's why. It's a changing of the guard. It happens every few centuries. Family infighting. They involve people from neighboring families who have been promised some little tidbit or other to help the wannabe head take power. It's a story as old as the vampires. Seems you and I got in the way."

Teaghan changed his destination. The enforcers probably knew which motel they'd used by now and might be lying in wait. He steered the car back onto the highway. If one family wanted him dead, then his only protection was to seek refuge in another family's territory.

While a risky proposition without petitioning for entrance first, the destination Teaghan had in mind came with a sponsor. He released Jeliyah's hand once more to bring up a number he hadn't called in years. He hoped it still worked.

"This is Mekhail. Who is this?"

"It's Teaghan, Mekhail. I'm calling in my favor." He tossed the phone back on the dash.

The man sighed into the phone in a resigned fashion. "What do you want?"

"Watch the tone. I want safe passage and a meeting with the family head to seek asylum for me and my necromancer."

"The head doesn't like necromancers."

"He likes them well enough to have two as his bodyguards."

"They are exceptions."

"You know what? I don't give a shit. I told you I'm calling in what's owed me. Make it happen. We'll be there in twenty hours or so."

Mekhail sighed again. "Yes, sire. Safe passage and a meeting. Does that make us even?"

"Depends on if we get asylum or not."

"I have no control over that."

"You better get some, then. Talk me up to the head or else your ass will be on the line to get us out of the territory and into the next safely. Get me?"

"Yes, sire. Call again when you near the border. I'll have escorts to meet you."

"Good." Teaghan ended the call.

Jeliyah asked, "Who was that? What favor does he owe you that he would vouch for us like that?"

"Mekhail is my progeny. Long story short—I made him after he'd been left for dead. He begged me to give him eternal life and to kill the ones who'd wronged him. I told him it would cost him and he agreed." He glanced at Jeliyah, meeting her haunted gaze. "He's in good with the head of the next territory over. We'll be safe."

"The vampire head who bought two platinum level necromancers and caused all that controversy. How can he not like necromancers and have two working for him?"

"Ask him when we get there." Teaghan pushed on the gas pedal, not worrying about cops. If he knew Fredrick and how the man operated, the local law enforcement had probably already been told the situation and warned to stay out of it.

Teaghan was heading west. "We can't head back to the motel."

"I figured as much already."

He smiled at the annoyance in her voice. Better mad than scared. He said, "Looks like you're going clothing shopping with me after all, necromancer."

"What about my money and yours? The jewels are in safe-deposit boxes back there." She waved over her shoulder.

"You can't still be worried about retirement?"

"No. But now that I know that money isn't going to the campus, I want it."

"Woman after my own heart." He raised her hand to his lips. "Don't worry, necromancer. Mekhail isn't the only one who owes me a favor. Once we're settled, I'll call in another solid to get our stashes."

"Do you put all your progeny in debt to you? You really are a mercenary. If you'd been born a necromancer, you would have made a great trustee." She snatched her hand away from him.

"Of the few progeny I have, only Mekhail is in debt to me. Everyone else in my ledger got in debt the old-fashioned way—they asked for a service and couldn't pay for it upfront."

"What service?"

"The kind I'm good at, killing people."

"How much am I going to owe you for saving my life?" She fixed him with a hard look. "Or are you going to put me down for a future favor?"

"I get that you're pissed, necromancer, but I'm not in the mood to be your whipping boy. We've got a long trip ahead of us. Get some sleep."

"What about you?"

"I fed deep tonight and can miss a day or two of rest before I start deteriorating. I can't say the same for you."

Jeliyah sat staring out the windshield for several breaths before she opened the glove box and took out her pouch of necromes. She put them on and flexed her fingers. "Activate."

Teaghan spared her a glance. "What're we dealing with?"

She closed her eyes. "Two following, though a fair distance back."

"Looks like we can relax, then. If Fredrick really wanted me dead and you captured, he would find some fabricated charge to slap me with rogue status. He's doing this on the down low for some reason."

"You wouldn't happen to have a friend in a high place, would you? Someone protecting you?"

"If I did, Fredrick wouldn't be up our asses now."

"Maybe Fredrick doesn't care if you're captured. He's probably figured out we're leaving the territory. That might be good enough for him, and the enforcers behind us are making sure."

"Smart thinking. You might be right. He probably figures we haven't had enough time to get proper permission to enter the next territory, meaning I would be killed and you would be captured the second we crossed the border." Teaghan sped up more. "Let's prove them wrong."

"Teaghan, are you sure Mekhail can get permission?"

"Owing a debt is more than an honor system with vampires, Jeliyah. We do blood pacts that put our lives at stake. If Mekhail doesn't do what I want, he'll die a very painful death by the magic binding us in contract to each other."

"Oh."

"Enough talk. Go to sleep. I'll wake you when I stop for gas so you can get some food."

"You're sure the enforcers won't attack us while you're refueling?"

"That's another reason why I'll be waking you. The blood might have weakened, but you still have enough of me in you to put up an impressive fight. The enforcers won't be so eager to attack when they realize that." He smoothed a finger down Jeliyah's cheek and said in a soothing tone, "Go to sleep, sweetness."

To help her along, he imagined the same babbling brook from the previous night and forced it into her mind, overshadowing her other thoughts. She didn't fight it and was eventually breathing peacefully in a deep slumber.

He stroked her cheek again, marveling at how completely she trusted him. Jeliyah didn't know the full extent of their connection. If Teaghan were the type, he could use the connection to make her do anything he wanted. Jeliyah's trustees had been wise to warn against sharing blood with a vampire because it was one step away from being a Renfield, despite what Teaghan had told her.

He had no plans to take advantage. He wanted Jeliyah to come to him on her own. The blood connection simply helped him understand her better and faster. They didn't have time for a normal courtship, not after being on the run—and not before either. Teaghan didn't have much patience.

Vampire or not, once he set his sights on something, he wanted it sooner rather than later and would use all means at his disposal to get it. He wanted Jeliyah more than anyone or anything before her. The situation surprised him, having never been confronted with it before, but he wouldn't deny it.

Once the current mess was settled and he could get back to seducing her, she wouldn't deny it, either.

CHAPTER
EIGHT

Jeliyah watched her necrome map shrink as their pursuers put more and more distance between them. She'd already mentioned the way the enforcers were backing off to Teaghan. He'd made a noncommittal noise to indicate he'd heard her, but hadn't offered an explanation. Not that she needed one.

She and Teaghan were close to the territory border. Teaghan had been driving the entire time, only stopping for gas. Vampires didn't get fatigued the way humans did, and they didn't fall prey to highway hypnosis. Almost a full day of driving hadn't affected Teaghan at all.

Jeliyah wasn't as resilient. She ached. The little sleep she had gotten—if sleep was what she wanted to call it—made her feel more exhausted than if she hadn't gotten any at all. Anxiety robbed her of her appetite and her irritability from low blood sugar had ended all conversation.

She startled when Teaghan placed his phone on the dash.

"Easy there, necromancer," Teaghan said with laughter.

The phone rang through the speakers.

Mekhail picked up after the second ring. "Are you here, sire?"

"Just about. We're ten miles out. Where's our escort meeting us?"

"The rest stop on the border. Pull in there. A black limo will be waiting to bring you the rest of the way. The head has agreed to meet you. In fact, he's eager to meet you. Almost too eager."

"You think it's a trap?"

"Not a trap. He assured me no harm would come to you or the necromancer during your stay, but wouldn't elaborate more than that. Several have said they haven't seen him this... enthusiastic in decades."

Jeliyah watched Teaghan to determine how she should react. She'd never met a vampire head. In fact, she doubted the trustees had met a vampire head either. The families guarded their leaders well. There was no way they would let a necromancer anywhere near. The exception being this vampire head, since he had necromancers for bodyguards.

Teaghan remained calm. "Good man, Mekhail. I need a limo ride after all this driving."

"Another will drive your car for you."

"Not needed. I'm dumping it."

Jeliyah had to hold back a surprised gasp. After all the bitching Teaghan had done about the bullet holes, she hadn't thought he would leave his car so easily.

"As you wish. I shall see you soon, sire."

"Yes, you will." Teaghan pressed the call end button and then glanced at her. "You already said I can buy a new car. You weren't wrong. And the car is deadweight we don't need."

"What about if the head decides we can't stay? How will we leave?"

"A limo waiting for us and he's enthusiastic. He's already decided to let us stay. It's on us whether or not we accept his terms."

"What terms?"

"We'll be finding out together." Teaghan threw the signal to show he was pulling off onto the exit.

As Mekhail said, a black stretch limo sat in the rest stop parking lot, out of place amongst the luggage-packed cars and campers. Two men—vampires from the way her necromes hummed louder—stood leaning against the car and watching the highway exit.

Teaghan pulled up alongside them. "Mekhail."

The men straightened, though neither claimed the name, nor greeted Teaghan the way Jeliyah thought a progeny would. She didn't know what she had expected, but nervous attention wasn't it.

One man pulled open the limo door. "Right this way, sir. The master is expecting you."

The other man rounded the car to Jeliyah's door and opened it for her. She was a little surprised when he offered his hand. She accepted since she wasn't sure of the steadiness of her legs.

All three men stood by while she entered the limo. Teaghan slid in after her. One escort closed the door, and both men went to the front of the limo.

She half expected to find someone waiting for them once her eyes adjusted to the darkness, but there was no one.

Teaghan pushed the talk button and asked, "How long?"

One escort said, "Four hours, sir. Did the miss need anything before we start?"

Jeliyah shook her head when Teaghan looked her way. She wanted this to be over with so she could go some place and truly relax.

"She's fine."

"Very good, sir."

The limo eased forward and got back on the highway. Jeliyah watched her map as the two dots that had been following them all day stayed in a spot that grew farther and farther away until they disappeared.

Teaghan said, "Power down and get some rest." He patted her thigh.

"I've been sleeping all day."

"No, you haven't. You've been watching the enforcers following us and needlessly expending energy. Stop arguing with me."

Jeliyah sighed, but decided to give in. He was right. She hadn't been sleeping, and she didn't feel up to playing diplomatic games while they bartered for asylum. "Deactivate."

Instead of using Teaghan's leg as a pillow, she slipped off the seat and stretched out over the floor of the limo, happy to extend her legs and flatten her back. Her muscles protested, but it was a good ache that made her groan in satisfaction.

Teaghan moved beside her and rolled her so her head rested on his shoulder. "Go to sleep," he whispered.

Jeliyah nodded. "Never thought this would be how I spent my first time in a limo." She sounded tired to her own ears. The noise of the highway passing underneath the car lulled her to sleep.

She woke to Teaghan's lips pressed against hers. She blinked up at him in surprise, but didn't pull away from the kiss.

He smiled down at her. "I've always wanted to do that."

"You haven't kissed a lover awake?"

"My lovers don't stick around long enough for me to wake them."

"Oh." Jeliyah thought about the women who had been hanging off Teaghan at the club. She couldn't imagine any of them being the type someone would want to wake up next to in the morning.

Teaghan sighed in annoyance. "I told you they are food, Jeliyah. That's it."

"You don't have to explain yourself to me." She sat up and climbed back onto the seat to look out the window. "Where are we? I have to assume we're close if you woke me."

A voice filtered over the intercom and said, "We are entering the property now, miss."

"Thank you." She looked at the talk button. She hadn't

needed to push it for the escorts to hear her question, though they had used it to answer. Teaghan had pressed it earlier when he could have skipped it, and she hadn't known why he bothered.

Teaghan said, "For you. I can hear them fine, but your ears are decidedly human."

That made sense, though she didn't say it out loud.

The limo stopped, and someone opened the door. Jeliyah took the hand offered, stepping out of the limo to look at the large estate nestled amongst the trees. She couldn't see much in the early morning darkness. Sunrise was still a few hours away.

The man holding her hand bowed over it and kissed her knuckles. "I am Mekhail, miss. Welcome to the home of Niccolo, head of the Amsel family."

"Thank you."

Behind her, Teaghan said, "You did well for yourself, Mekhail."

"Thank you, sire." Mekhail gestured to the house. "A room, clothing, and refreshments have been prepared for you. Niccolo will see you in an hour."

Jeliyah was happy she didn't have to meet with someone as important as Niccolo without seeing the inside of a shower first. Niccolo probably didn't want to meet them before they showered, anyway. She wished they could postpone until she'd slept a little longer, though.

The room Mekhail showed them was large and ornate, with a four-poster bed, complete with canopy and curtains, a matching vanity, and a lounging sofa. The room also had a young woman— early twenties at the most—waiting.

Mekhail said, "I did not know the nature of your relationship, miss, so assumed Teaghan would require a food source other than you. I hope I didn't overstep myself."

Jeliyah smiled at him. "No, you didn't. Thank you. And she's just Teaghan's type too."

"I know it well, miss. I used to procure women for him in the days before the outing." His gaze swept over her. "You would not have been on my list."

Teaghan snapped, "And that's enough out of you." He pointed to the door.

Mekhail kissed Jeliyah's hand again and nodded to Teaghan before leaving the room. Teaghan slammed the door after him, making the girl jump with a surprised squeak.

Jeliyah said to her, "He's grumpy from our long trip. Don't let his attitude scare you. He won't hurt you."

The girl smiled. "I'm—"

"Don't care," Teaghan growled. To Jeliyah, he said, "Take the shower first."

"Thanks. I won't be long."

"Take as long as you want. I can be quick."

Vampire—of course he could. Jeliyah decided not to question it. She gathered up the neatly folded clothes, a towel and a basket filled with feminine toiletries—there was another basket with men's products—and went to the bathroom.

She stayed in the shower until her fingers pruned, taking Teaghan at his word that he didn't need that long. The dress Niccolo supplied her, while floor-length and made of opaque material, matched something Teaghan might have chosen. The front dipped to her navel, revealing the swells of her breasts. A thin chain ladder kept the two halves from falling open.

The same style chain ladder connected the front panel of the skirt to the back. A skirt that left the sides of her legs bare from the waist down. The person who chose her clothes hadn't felt the need to include underwear. She wasn't fond of thongs, but would have appreciated a pair because her panties would be seen if she wore them. She had to go without. That made her more than a little self-conscious.

She exited the bathroom to find the girl gone and Teaghan staring out the window. He faced her before she could say anything. His gaze as he looked her over heated her skin. Her thoughts went back to the previous night—had so little time passed?—and her pussy twitched in reaction.

"Very nice," he said in a low rumble.

She said quickly, "You have to shower."

Teaghan grinned. "I hadn't planned to do otherwise." He crossed the room in the time it took her to blink and said with his mouth close to her neck, "But I will do everything you just thought of later." After a soft kiss against her shoulder, he disappeared into the bathroom.

She didn't have time to get herself under control because Teaghan emerged five minutes later, clothed in a suit and with his hair damp. She liked this look better on him. Even with his hair still in cornrows, he looked dapper and dangerous.

"Really?" He glanced down at himself. "I might have to buy a few then, since this one seems to have gotten you all hot and bothered."

Jeliyah didn't try to deny it. Teaghan could hear her thoughts, so there was no point.

A knock drew both of their attentions to the door. Mekhail entered. "The master is ready to see you now." He smiled at Jeliyah. "You look beautiful, miss."

"Thank you."

He offered her his elbow. "Shall we?"

She started to put her hand on his arm, but Teaghan stuck out his elbow on her other side. He said in a rough tone, "Yes, we shall."

Jeliyah took his arm to keep a fight from breaking out.

Mekhail didn't appear to mind. He turned and led the way to a library with bookshelves built into the walls. A man who appeared to be in his forties sat at the large desk situated in the middle of the room. Two secret-service-looking men—black suits, earpieces, and stiff attitudes—flanked him.

The man at the desk said, "I am Niccolo, head of the Amsel family. You are Jeliyah Parsons, palladium level necromancer, and

Teaghan, an enforcer. Sit." He gestured to the two chairs across from the desk. "Mekhail, you're dismissed."

Teaghan handed Jeliyah down to one chair and sat on his after moving it closer to her.

Mekhail left the room, closing the door after.

Only then did Niccolo speak. "I understand you got in the way of a family head transition."

Teaghan said, "If I'd known that was the deal, I would have taken my necromancer back to the motel and holed up there the rest of the night like they wanted. It's not my style to interfere with politics. I leave that to the ambitious sorts."

Niccolo nodded. "Yes. I requested your record before granting your petition. You are quite the impressive enforcer. Very dedicated. A born killer, as one person annotated in your file." He tapped the file in question, which sat on the desk in front of him.

"I never said otherwise. If they didn't want the rogue killed, they should have never told me about him."

"I agree. That was stupid on their parts." Niccolo turned his gaze to Jeliyah. "You are new to the field and yet have broken every rule of your training from almost the first day."

Jeliyah didn't know what to say. She couldn't deny it and didn't know how he knew.

The man smiled. "I like that about you. It's the reason I granted you asylum. You intrigue me. Few necromancers would go against years of conditioning to willingly sample a vampire's blood."

"How did you know?" Too late, she realized her question might be revealing too much.

Niccolo held up one file. "Your campus wants you back badly. They sent out bulletins detailing your transgressions, along with a sizable reward to the one who delivers you."

Jeliyah swallowed back the tears that threatened to precede her pleading for her life.

"Take heart, my dear. No amount of money would entice me

into giving you to those jackals. Neither will they enter my territory to try to take you. You are safe here."

"Thank you, sire."

"Call me Niccolo. I am no royalty. I got this position after I killed my predecessor, which is why I took on Machiavelli's name." He tented his fingers with a slow smile curving his lips. "I want to tell you both a story. It's my story, and it will explain why I'm helping you. That way Teaghan stops acting like I will attack you at any moment."

Jeliyah glanced at Teaghan, who sat back in his seat with a bored air. She guessed Niccolo's vampire eyes could see something she couldn't. She didn't hear anything from Teaghan's thoughts, either. Not that the lack surprised her. He could block.

Niccolo said, "I was once known as Reginald Van Helsing." His smile grew at Jeliyah's loud gasp, and he nodded. "I see my family's reputation remains well known."

"Yes, sir," Jeliyah whispered in awe. "The history books said your family was killed."

"After a while, yes, we were. But only after a while. The necromancer families came after us for my uncle's part in the making of Bram Stoker's book. They gave us to the vampires for punishment, specifically to Ulrike, who was the head of the Amsel family at the time. She made us all Renfields to toy with at her leisure. I was her favorite." He paused and rubbed the bridge of his nose. "Every time I displeased her, she killed a member of my family—brutally and without compassion."

"I'm sorry."

"This is long before your birth, my dear. You have nothing to be sorry for. The last of my family to die was my twin sister Regan. Ulrike thought I conspired against her, so she had my sister raped and mutilated before ripping off her head in front of me."

Jeliyah covered her mouth, muffling her horrified gasp.

"The conspiracy Ulrike imagined was a surprise birthday party. When she learned that truth, she shrugged away her actions with a halfhearted apology and permission to bury my sister. As though I needed permission. After that day, I courted her favor in all things, making her think I loved her. The day after she granted me vampirism, I used my new strength to rip off her head and claim her spot as ruler of this family.

"Of course I was challenged, but none could stand against me. The Van Helsings were all platinum level necromancers to a one. It's funny to note that necromancers retain their abilities, whether we become Renfields or vampires. The negating powers of the necromes don't affect us. I think it is because of our blood or our chromosomes, or possibly both. And you, my dear, have firsthand knowledge of what vampire blood can do to your abilities. It is more so for Renfields and vampires."

Teaghan said, "This is a great story, but what's it got to do with us?"

"I hate the necromancers' guild—now called trustees—for their part in the massacre of my family. My uncle's punishment for his crime shouldn't have carried to us all. It was a cover. They used a small infraction to act on their petty jealousies. The Van Helsing line always produced platinum level and palladium level offspring. Once, we even produced a rhodium level."

Jeliyah gasped again. "The history books never mentioned that. They're so rare that the books should mention it even if the Van Helsings were ousted."

"Jealousy, my dear. Plain and simple. We were the best, with the strongest and most consistent bloodline, and the others hated us for it. The vampires couldn't have cared less about Stoker's book. Similar tales had been spun for centuries without chance of an outing, but Ulrike didn't want to pass up the chance of having new toys."

"She did the trustees' dirty work," Jeliyah said.

"She made them think she had. She was supposed to kill us all and told them she had. Instead, she made us Renfields to use our powers as a way to reinforce her position."

97

Teaghan said, "Smart woman."

"She was." Niccolo pushed the two folders containing Jeliyah's and Teaghan's information aside. "As to Teaghan's earlier question, given my past, I am happy to keep Jeliyah safe from the trustees. Of course, that means Teaghan can stay as well."

Jeliyah relaxed, barely keeping herself from sliding off her chair in a grateful puddle. "Thank you, sir. Thank you so much."

"Provided you can prove you have truly broken your conditioning."

She stiffened once more. "How do I do that?"

Niccolo gestured to Teaghan. "Under him or beside him. Your choice."

"Excuse me?"

Teaghan said while holding Niccolo's gaze, "He means as my Renfield or as my progeny."

"What?!" Jeliyah didn't mean to yell and didn't excuse her tone.

Niccolo didn't appear bothered. "The outing gave the trustees what they needed to extend the power of their cult—enticing young, impressionable youths with limitless credit cards while indoctrinating them to be good little acolytes. You are no different, Jeliyah."

"I—"

"How much is your balance, Jeliyah? What must you give them to retire? A word we both know doesn't mean what it should."

Jeliyah felt the trap closing around her. She whispered, "There has to be another way."

"There isn't."

"Please?"

"I refuse. You want my help, and this is the price. Do not think you can go to another territory and receive better. They would hand you over to the trustees the second you made yourself known. I am your only option, and I demand you prove yourself. I will not suffer a necromancer in my midst just to be stabbed in the back when the trustees offer an adequate lure."

Jeliyah looked at the men flanking Niccolo. They showed no reaction to the situation. That wasn't right. "What about them? They're necromancers."

Niccolo spared them a glance. "They are Renfields and have been since they came into my employ. The trustees don't know that and won't figure it out for another few decades."

"Willing Renfields?" Teaghan asked.

"Very willing. You see, these two gentlemen went quite wild when given their credit cards after entering the campus. The campus treated them like royalty because they are both platinum level. This one—" he pointed to the man on his left "—bought a top-of-the-line sports car with all the options. By the time he graduated, his retirement price was well into the hundreds of millions. The other is no different. They were doomed to a life of paying off their debts like a common yellow gold, hunting rogues since no one thought they were worth their debt, even as platinums. I made them the same offer I'm putting to you, Jeliyah. Come to me as a Renfield or a vampire, and I'll make it all better."

Jeliyah said, "Define all better."

Niccolo picked up her folder and held it out to the man on his right.

The man walked it to the fire across the room and tossed it in.

Niccolo said, "Your debt cleared, your transgressions bribed into nonexistence, and the freedom to do as you please with the rest of your immortal life. Death is the only way the trustees will free you, Jeliyah. I offer you the choice of how you will die."

She fought to keep her breathing steady when all she wanted to do was hyperventilate because of the panic spreading over her. Teaghan and Niccolo had to hear the thundering of her heart beating against her rib cage. She couldn't do this.

"I know you're scared, my dear. That is the years of brainwashing clawing to retain control. Push it aside the way you did when you took Teaghan's blood, the way you did when you invited him to take your body." Niccolo stood and rounded the desk. He stopped in front of Jeliyah's chair. Stooping down, he caught her gaze and said, "Very little changes. I promise you. Necromancers and vampires are made from the same magic. We are opposites on the same coin. You know that, don't you?"

She nodded, unable to speak.

"Good. That might be the reason you can fight their conditioning. Don't stop halfway. Take the last step and break their control completely."

Teaghan moved to her side, placed his hand on her shoulder, and said to Niccolo, "She needs time to think about this."

Niccolo stood and backed up a few steps. "Of course. I hadn't expected her to decide right away." He returned to his seat. "You have twenty-four hours to prove you want to be free, or else I'll give you to the trustees myself."

Jeliyah stared at him in disbelief. Twenty-four hours amounted to no time at all. How could he expect her to make such a heavy decision so quickly?

Teaghan asked, "What about me, Niccolo?"

The man waved dismissively. "You are free to stay or go as you please, enforcer. Mekhail has vouched for you, but I have no need for your services. Jeliyah is not the first necromancer to hear my ultimatum. Quite a few of the vampires in my territory are former necromancers. It's the reason we don't need enforcers."

"How?" Jeliyah asked in a hoarse tone. "The trustees would have noticed necromancers coming to this territory and never returning."

"Who said they belonged to the trustees? They aren't the only ones able to locate and recruit young necromancers as they come of age. My territory has no campus. I ousted the one that was here after usurping Ulrike. Any recruiter coming here chances death. The necromancers born in this territory must be trained, so I provide that service. Unlike your campus, I teach of the similarities between vampires and necromancers and have my trainees taste vampire blood as part of their training. There is no one below gold level amongst my students. And all choose to be changed after they graduate, or they leave to take their chances outside."

Niccolo stood again. "But enough of this. I am wasting the time you need to decide. This time tomorrow, you will come to me changed, or you will leave chained. Decide if your loyalty to the trustees is worth what they'll do to you if they get you back."

Teaghan helped Jeliyah stand. She used his arm to keep herself upright as they walked back to their room. She saw nothing except the choice Niccolo gave her.

While she understood his hatred of the trustees, why force her to make this decision? There had to be another way to show she had broken her ties with her former caretakers. They wanted her back so they could bleed her and worse. She would be an idiot to want to return.

"Then let me change you," Teaghan said in a low voice as he closed the bedroom door.

Jeliyah met his gaze with a disbelieving one. "What?"

"Niccolo won't bend his one rule for you. Don't try him and think he will. He's right to demand this. I've seen your world, Jeliyah. It's a cult, like he said. All the trustees have to do is offer a shiny enough carrot and you'll go back to them."

"I won't!"

"You will. That's what you've been trained to do. I can hear your thoughts, Jeliyah. Every decision you make is based on the lessons they taught you. You took my blood and invited me into your body and then tortured yourself with images of what the trustees would do if they found out."

She wanted to cover her ears to block out his words. Her emotions teetered on the edge of sending her into a spiraling abyss of depression. This wasn't safety.

"It can be." Teaghan framed her face with his hands. "Come to my side, Jeliyah. Be with me."

"You mean under you," she snapped, pulling out of his hold.

His answering grin made her itch to smack the expression off his face.

"I don't want to make you my Renfield, Jeliyah. But I do want you under me. On top of me, too. You ride me so well."

"This is nothing but sex to you. This is my life," she screamed.

"Then prove it," Teaghan said in a normal tone. "Let me change you. Claim a life that will be completely yours. No more debt. No more waiting for the campus to give you new orders and work you into an early grave. No grave at all." He pulled her into his arms and held her as she struggled. "Don't fight this, Jeliyah. You know the decision you must make. You wouldn't have run if you were the type to accept punishment easily."

"I need more time."

"No, you don't. The choices won't change in twenty-four hours or twenty-four days."

She tasted the salt of her tears before she realized she was crying. This was too hard. Why did freedom have to come at such a high price?

"It always does," Teaghan whispered, hugging her close and patting the back of her head. "Prove you're worth it. Choose freedom and a future you've made for yourself."

"Why are you waiting for me to say yes? You could just do it, and I wouldn't have any say in the matter."

"I won't. I'm not letting you make me a scapegoat, Jeliyah." He pulled her back so she met his gaze. "I'm also not letting you martyr yourself for some warped ideal based on misplaced loyalty."

"You're contradicting yourself."

"I'm letting you know the deal before I start convincing you to make the right decision."

"Convincing me how?"

His grin should have been her warning, but her turbulent emotions blinded her to the situation. She figured it out when he started snapping the chains holding the front halves of her dress together.

CHAPTER
NINE

Teaghan loosened his hold so he could divest Jeliyah of her dress. Rather than unhook the chains, he broke them, and she stared up at him as he did it, not stopping him.

He knew she was struggling with a tough decision, or he gathered she felt it was tough. When it had been Teaghan making the choice, he'd embraced it readily. Immortality meant he could continue killing people far into the future. Vampirism meant he would be more efficient at it.

There had been other enticements, but those two meant the most to him.

Jeliyah wasn't him. She needed something other than her own life to tip the scale toward vampirism, and he knew just the something to give her.

Her breasts popped free when he snapped the last chain at the collar of the dress. He beheld the twin mounds of delicious perfection and couldn't decide which should get his attention first.

His indecision gave Jeliyah enough time to break away from him and stalk toward the door.

She snapped, "This won't help me."

"I beg to differ." Teaghan chased after her, staying one step behind her until she got to the door. He pinned her there with his chest pressed against her back. "Vampires have heightened senses, Jeliyah."

"I know that."

"You're aware of it, but won't know the truth until you choose to be changed." He snapped three of the chains on the side of her dress so he could slip his hand under the front flap. He trailed his fingers through the tight curls covering her mons before going lower to tap her clit.

Jeliyah's breathing caught. She pressed into his hand, trapping it between herself and the door.

"Sex was an interesting pastime while I was human. It became an obsession after my change. Heightened senses don't mean just hearing, sight, and smell. Touch and taste are included in that." He switched to rubbing her clit in small circles that her hips mimicked. Whispering in her ear, he said, "Imagine this sensation magnified by three, maybe four. A simple touch—" he squeezed the tiny nub, making Jeliyah keen with need "—could send you into orgasm. It takes years to acclimate to the new sensitivity of your skin after the change."

"This won't—" She pulled in a shuddering breath and scraped her fingers along the door. "Life is about more than sex, Teaghan." She pushed back against him, probably to shove him away, but all she did was rub her ass against the bulge in his pants.

He moved forward so she could feel more of his arousal. "Life is about many things, pleasure top amongst them. Your trustees can't offer you that."

"You're spewing the same nonsense they did when they recruited me." This time, when she shoved against him, she made him back up. She escaped to the side, looking frazzled and cornered even though she had the large room surrounding her. "Credit cards without a limit. Amazing sex. It's all hollow when weighed against my life. No matter what I choose, someone will own me."

"I don't want to own you, Jeliyah."

"Then help me."

"I am."

"No, you aren't!" Her gaze went to the window.

Teaghan didn't bother looking. She wasn't seeing the scenery, but the illusion of freedom she thought existed beyond the windows. "Leave without being changed and you're in for a world of pain, necromancer. You know that."

"I... I..." She shook her head hard. "Why did you bring me here?"

"I want you safe."

"Dead isn't safe."

Teaghan rushed her. He grabbed her against his chest and held her, though she fought to free herself. With one arm around her waist, he used the other to force one of her hands against his chest. "Feel that. That's a heartbeat, Jeliyah. I'm not dead."

She stared at her hand. "A corpse animated by magic that forces blood through your veins so you can play human."

"Fine. I'm a magic corpse, but you're the same, necromancer. You said it. Niccolo did too. You're alive, but you're not human. Vampires and necromancers are two sides of the same magic. The only difference is I had to die before mine took effect. You've been this way since birth."

He felt the realization hit her. She stared at him with wide, spooked eyes. Teaghan knew he had to get her past this, past the idea that everything would be okay if she held on to her notion of living. It wouldn't. Niccolo wasn't bluffing. The trustees sure as hell weren't either.

He released her and then smoothed his fingers down her cheek. "Be changed, Jeliyah. Be with me. You've seen my life. I live. I'm alive. You'll still be a necromancer, but you'll also have the power of a vampire to back it up. You felt a bit of that when you tasted my blood. Take the last step."

She whispered in a voice that sounded as if it belonged to a child, "I don't want to die."

The vulnerability in those few words tore at Teaghan's heart. He couldn't calm that fear. In order to be a vampire, she had to die. Mortal death, but still death. He didn't want to be the one to kill her, though he trusted no one else to do it, to help her through the change.

He laid a soft kiss on her lips. "I'll be right here, sweetness. I'll bring you back. Promise. I've done it many times already. I know what I'm doing."

Silent tears trailed down her cheeks. She was giving in and the decision scared the hell out of her. This wasn't breaking free of brainwashing that wanted to retain its hold, but simple human survival instinct.

"Please?"

He framed her face with both hands. "What, sweetness?"

"I don't want to die. Please, Teaghan. Please." She gripped his hands as desperation entered her eyes. "Living like that is death. I don't want to die."

The image of the bleeding room flitted across her mind. The memory of IVs siphoning off blood to create necro-metal and a room that smelled overwhelmingly of sterilizers was the reason Jeliyah hated hospitals today.

The tension surrounding Teaghan's heart loosened as he realized what she was saying. He gave her a sad smile. "Say it, Jeliyah. You have to say it. Invite me."

She swallowed loud and wet her lips before she said, "Make me a vampire, Teaghan."

"With pleasure." He pulled her to him and kissed her sweet lips, happier than he thought he would be at hearing her say the words. It was for his own peace of mind. He'd already been invited into her body and didn't need another invitation to change her. But he didn't want her looking back on this day and thinking he'd forced her.

He would have. He wouldn't lie to himself. Jeliyah wouldn't have left this room a human. Teaghan had been prepared to make her a Renfield if she refused to make a choice either way. She would have hated him for that, and he'd been prepared to take it because he knew they would have time enough together for him to earn her forgiveness.

Now that wasn't needed.

He lifted her into his arms and carried her to the bed. Her kittenish sound of surprise when he yanked her dress off made his dick twitch.

"Teaghan?"

"Relax, sweetness. I plan to change you. But first, let's bid goodbye to your humanity."

Her heart rate increased. To his amazement, Jeliyah spread her legs and reached for him, opening herself and inviting him in the most seductive way possible.

He tore off his suit and joined her on the bed.

Jeliyah hugged him close with her legs wrapped around his waist and her arms around his shoulders. The slick heat of her slit teased the tip of his erection. Teaghan held back the urge to enter her. Not yet.

He coaxed her to free her hold on him so he could get to her breasts. The twin beauties had been calling to him since Jeliyah bound them in that dress. Free now, her breasts lay bare for his perusal. He watched them sway and quiver with each breath she took and every beat of her heart.

A heart he would soon stop so that magic could restart it. Teaghan didn't want to think about that at this moment. He latched on to one of Jeliyah's pert nipples to distract himself. She cooed beneath him and shifted. He had to lift his waist away to keep her from pulling his dick into that tight pussy of hers.

Jeliyah whimpered and tried to follow him.

He pressed one hand to her belly and held her down.

"Teaghan," she said in a breathy tone full of need.

He smiled around her nipple, but didn't give her what she wanted. Instead, he slipped one finger between her lower lips so he could rub her clit.

Jeliyah cried out as she arched, pressing her nipple farther into his mouth.

He sucked at the offering and enjoyed the way she moaned in reaction. Jeliyah had a sensitive body. Teaghan could see years of acclimation sex on the horizon for them before she grew accustomed to her heightened vampire senses.

Teaghan almost laughed at himself. Years. He'd never contemplated weeks with one woman, let alone years. Jeliyah made him wish for decades, centuries. He wanted to indulge the sweet aroma of her aloe-and-cucumber-scented skin mixed with the musk of her lust for as long as he had the ability to smell it.

He inhaled as he switched to her other nipple and flicked it with his tongue. The bud grew stiff with the attention he gave it, and Jeliyah moaned louder. When he slid two fingers past her pulsing entrance, filling her channel, she wrapped her arms around his head and held him tight to her breasts.

Her hips rose off the bed to meet his thrusting fingers. Her mind begged him for his dick, for a deeper penetration than his fingers could provide.

Teaghan wanted to give in to the request, but there was a method to the madness to which he subjected her.

Leaving her nipple, he trailed kisses down between her breasts and over her belly. He had to shift his position so he was beside her instead of between her legs, but Jeliyah didn't protest. She continued writhing as his fingers teased her inside.

He laid a kiss on her clit.

"Oh!" Jeliyah's legs quaked.

Teaghan gave her tiny nub another kiss before lapping at it. It didn't take many licks before Jeliyah vocalized her release loud enough that Teaghan was sure many, if not all, the vampires in the estate heard her.

He kept her trapped in the feeling with the fingers of one hand churning her pussy while the other hand rubbed her clit, distracting her from the pain of him pricking her inner thigh with his fangs. He pierced her femoral artery and drank deep before retreating from the wound so it bled freely.

This was the part Teaghan didn't like. The death Jeliyah feared so much. He chose this way to make it as painless for her as possible. The rapid beat of her heart from their activity sped up her blood loss.

He stopped teasing her as her breathing slowed along with her heartbeat.

"Teaghan?" A little fear tinged her voice.

He stretched out along her side so she could feel his heat. "Right here, sweetness. Right here."

"I... I..." She took several deep breaths before she sighed her last.

Teaghan clenched his fists, holding back the urge to shake her, to call her back. That wasn't how it was done. He had to wait. The longest minutes of his life passed while he watched Jeliyah.

The waiting had never seemed so bad before this moment. It was a few minutes. No time at all and yet Teaghan struggled to keep his cool. Too soon, and he would be making her a Renfield—alive, tied to his life, and a slave. Too late, and he would be making her a tombstone. It was all about timing.

Then he felt it.

A tiny tickle across his senses.

The spark of life.

Jeliyah's life.

Her consciousness split from her body, preparing to move on to the hereafter. That was the signal he'd been waiting for. He dragged a fingernail down his wrist before holding it over her mouth. With his free hand, he massaged her throat so she swallowed.

He stared at the wound he'd given her, willing it to close. A relieved smile curved his lips when the twin holes on her inner thigh grew skin as they healed. His bite left behind two sunken scars. The only remnants of the wound he'd made to change her. The last scars she would ever carry.

Cupping her head, Teaghan kissed Jeliyah's lips. Soft at first. A simple reassurance she was coming back to him. Her mouth moved beneath his and he deepened the kiss, slipping his tongue over hers.

Jeliyah inhaled as she circled her arms around his shoulders and returned his kiss.

"Welcome back," he whispered.

Jeliyah blinked at him, confusion playing across her features. "Back?"

"Don't worry if you don't remember. Most don't." He kissed her again so she wouldn't dwell on it. There was no need to remember death when he wanted to revel in life.

He rolled so he was on his back and Jeliyah was on top of him.

She still appeared confused. "Teaghan, did you do it? Am I—" She winced and touched her lip. A drop of blood appeared there before the wound closed. She'd bitten her lip with her new canines. "I..." She trailed off and touched one of her fangs.

Teaghan pulled her hand away. "Worry about that later. I've got something else for you to poke yourself with." He rolled his hips, sliding his dick low across her belly.

Jeliyah's eyes widened and darkened as hunger overtook her uncertainty. It was a hunger Teaghan shared, so he rubbed his arousal against her mons to whet her appetite.

She let her legs fall open, straddled him, then slid back. Her hot pussy enveloped Teaghan's erection and a deep rumbling growl of satisfaction left her throat, startling her into covering her mouth while she stared at him with wide eyes.

"Yeah, that was you. Now get over it and move." He bucked, driving to her depths in one stroke.

He wasn't trying to be insensitive to her new situation. Okay, he was, but he was hurting. The soft heat surrounding his dick made him want to roll Jeliyah over and pound her sweet slit until they were both growling their pleasure. He stayed on his back with her on top so she could control the encounter. It was his one concession to the fact that she had changed and sex would be more acute for her.

He thrust again.

Jeliyah used the momentum to lift away from him until only his tip was treated to her softness. As though entering a boiling tub of water, Jeliyah lowered herself slowly, hesitantly. Her breath came in hitches as she took his length back into her pussy.

The long sigh that left her lips once she had him fully inside her again feathered across Teaghan's chest. He was glad she could relax because he was ready to snap. When she moved again, clenching her inner muscles, squeezing his dick as she lifted up, he dug his fingers into the bed to keep from grabbing her and forcing her to go faster.

Jeliyah returned quicker than she left. The third time, her pace increased again. She panted with her face pressed against his chest as she rocked her hips. Each motion was slow. Testing. Teasing. Driving him crazy, but he took it. All the while he thought of the babbling brook he used to keep Jeliyah calm, sharing the thought with her, though it was mostly for him.

He sucked in a breath when she trailed light kisses over the scar on his chest. She moved her mouth to his neck. Her new fangs scraped his skin, lingering over the throbbing vein there. His dick jumped, making Jeliyah squeak at the thought of her biting him. A nibble made sex better for vampires. She continued her kisses to his ear, and he figured she might not be ready for that just yet.

She brushed her lips across the edge of his mouth on her way to pressing her cheek against his. Fisting her hands where they rested on his chest, she rolled her lower body. A loud whimper of pleasure left her lips, and she shuddered before she did it again.

Teaghan stayed still, liking this new torture. Except it didn't stay torture for long.

Jeliyah caught the rhythm quickly. She circled her hips as she rocked her body, riding his dick. He couldn't help moving with her until the entire bed shook side to side with the force of their combined motions.

Faster and harder. Harder and faster. Jeliyah alternated between panting moans and hungry growling. Her nails raked along his chest, which Teaghan loved. Her momentum kept building until Teaghan had to rest a hand on the small of her back. He pressed her down, while lifting himself up, to slow her. She was tapping into her vampiric speed at the wrong time. And that was a lesson for later.

He turned his head to capture her lips as he took control of the pace, bouncing beneath her.

Jeliyah whimpered into his mouth. Her whole body tightened, squeezing his dick, as she came.

"Love you," she said, panting. "Love you."

The hum of her necromes startled Teaghan and threw off his pace. She hadn't taken them off when she changed to meet Niccolo. Teaghan didn't know why they were activating now, possibly something to do with her new existence as a vampire.

Since they wouldn't sap the magic from his body and turn him into a lifeless lump, he ignored the sound to focus on Jeliyah and to make sure her first moments as a vampire were memorable. That meant multiple orgasms.

She rose to a sitting position with her hands braced on his chest and met his thrusts. Teaghan cupped her ass, kneading and guiding her. He could feel her heading toward another climax while he neared his first.

The necromes hummed louder. The vibration of the metal echoed through him from Jeliyah. Whatever it was, it felt fantastic.

Teaghan had never known a necromancer's power could create pleasure.

He opened his mouth to say so. Instead, he said in unison with Jeliyah, "Resonate."

Their gazes locked. Teaghan couldn't look away and didn't want to. The force of the spell weaving around them kept him and Jeliyah moving, satisfying each other until they peaked together. He lifted his hips off the bed as the force of his release seemed to drain all his strength into Jeliyah.

She shook and her inner muscles clenched around him, trying to milk more of what he didn't have. As though her pussy realized there was nothing left and Teaghan had given all he could, Jeliyah relaxed. She collapsed against his chest with a satisfied purr.

Teaghan held her there as he eased out of her. After a little adjusting, he situated Jeliyah so she curved around his side. He liked her in that position. She hugged his waist and kissed his chest with a contented sigh that Teaghan echoed.

The hard part was over. Everything that followed was adjustment.

CHAPTER

TEN

Jeliyah didn't feel right. And by right, she meant the way she had gotten used to feeling for the last twenty-seven years.

"You'll adjust. You have to relearn how to move," Teaghan said.

"Joy," she bit out, almost biting her tongue. Her new canines took some getting used to as well. She had to learn to talk around them without sounding as if she had a mouth full of cotton. "I don't like that you can still hear my thoughts. I'm a vampire, not a Renfield."

"Blame yourself for that. As soon as you changed, the connection should have closed. This is all necromancer. Probably something to do with Resonate."

She shook her head. "I don't know what that is or how I knew how to cast it."

"We'll ask Niccolo."

After sleeping the day away, they were on their way to Niccolo's office to show Jeliyah's choice. It was a few hours before the deadline, but neither she nor Teaghan wanted to delay, given the strange things that had been happening since her change.

One of Niccolo's Renfields opened the door to his office before they could knock. Niccolo sat at his desk, wearing a knowing grin. "How do you feel, my dear?"

"Weird."

He nodded and gestured to the empty chairs. "That's to be expected. You need to learn how your body has changed—and hasn't."

Jeliyah sat before asking, "What's Resonate? Have you heard of it?"

"Resonate. Why would you want to know about such an old, banned spell?"

She and Teaghan exchanged a look. He shrugged. She turned her attention back to Niccolo and said, "I cast it without meaning to after Teaghan turned me. Actually, we both cast it."

Niccolo's eyes widened. "Why would you do that?"

"We didn't do it on purpose." She gestured to her rings. "I was still wearing them and we…" She shifted as her thoughts turned to her first experience as a vampire. "I was still wearing them when the change happened. I cast before I knew what I was saying."

"Resonate is a rare spell and shouldn't be anything to worry about. It doesn't work unless used on a vampire on whom the necromancer has already used Recognize."

"I have," Jeliyah said.

At the same time, Teaghan said, "She has."

Niccolo pulled back. "Excuse me?"

Jeliyah said, "The day I took Teaghan's blood, I cast Recognize. It was the only way I could think to help him from afar without hitting him."

"You cast Recognize *after* taking his blood?"

She didn't know why he emphasized it the way he had, but she nodded. "Yes. Why? That's how Recognize is cast."

Niccolo chuckled. "I doubt your campus taught you Recognize. How did you learn of it?"

"After it was found that I couldn't get pregnant, I had a lot of free time for self-study. I spent my days in the library. That was how I learned about the Van Helsings—or what the books say about your family—and random spells not taught in class."

"Such as?"

"Ghost Status, Recognize, and a few others. Given what the spells do, it didn't surprise me they were never taught. The books where I found them were in the old language, which isn't taught either. I spent a lot of time self-teaching it so I could read the books. I also didn't let on what all I learned."

"Smart girl. It seems you broke your mind control earlier than I thought. Perhaps if they hadn't cast you aside after finding out you couldn't reproduce, you might not be here today."

Jeliyah shrugged. "I'm not one to speculate about different pasts and how they would change the future."

Niccolo stood and came around the desk. Taking one of Jeliyah's hands in his, he said, "Let me educate you, my dear. Recognize and Resonate are from the days when necromancers and vampires weren't enemies."

"When the fuck was that? I'm almost three hundred and don't remember anything like that," Teaghan said.

Niccolo nodded. "It's older than that, enforcer. I told you already. Necromancers and vampires are two sides of the same magical coin. Almost like siblings. There was a time when we didn't hate each other. Near the beginning when spells like Recognize and Resonate were used freely." He smiled at them in turn. "Between mates."

"What?!" Jeliyah and Teaghan said in unison.

Their shocked synchronization set Niccolo laughing. He indulged his mirth for a few minutes before pulling in a deep breath and calming himself to talk. "Forgive me. Had I known you had cast Recognize after tasting Teaghan's blood, I wouldn't have forced vampirism on you, Jeliyah."

Jeliyah asked in a chilled tone, "What?"

"You tied yourself to Teaghan that day."

"But that... the spell is so my necromes can't harm him."

"True, but blood isn't needed to do that."

"What? But the book... the book said blood..." Her mind raced as she tried to remember what she had read. Had she overlooked something or mistranslated?

A familiar babbling brook coursed through her mind. She looked at Teaghan, who gave her a sad smile. "Calm down, Jeliyah. Listen to Niccolo."

She pulled in several deep breaths. To Niccolo, she said, "Explain, please."

Niccolo said, "What you wanted to do—your necromes bringing no harm to Teaghan—didn't require blood. Recognize is two different spells by the same name. Without blood, it gives the target vampire immunity from all necromes made with your blood. With blood, it does the same but also forges a bond between the two of you. A bond you completed when you cast Resonate."

"A bond," she said in a monotone.

"Yes. Your sexual relationship started shortly after Recognize, did it not?"

She nodded.

"I've heard Teaghan can be quite persuasive to the opposite sex, but a campus-raised necromancer should have been able to resist. Am I right? Were you even remotely interested in him prior to Recognize?"

"Watch it," Teaghan snapped.

Jeliyah thought back. She'd cast Recognize the second day. The first day, she hadn't cared if her spells took out Teaghan and the rogue at the same time. Only her life being in danger had changed that. She said, "Not really."

Niccolo shrugged. "Don't feel too bad."

"But..." She glanced at Teaghan. Was their entire relationship because of some spell?

"Recognize after blood doesn't work on just any necromancer and vampire. In case you're wondering. I've spent long years studying the old texts from the days of unity—that's what I call it.

A necromancer and a vampire wishing to forge the bond of Recognize and Resonate have to have an existing connection."

"I just met him five days ago."

"The connection I speak of is spiritual. A meeting of souls, if you will. Humans call it love at first sight."

"I hated him the second I laid eyes on him."

Teaghan snorted.

Niccolo said, "There's a thin line between love and hate. That line gave you the ability to cast Recognize after tasting his blood and forced you to cast Resonate when your feelings aligned."

Jeliyah found that vampires could blush when her cheeks heated. The memory of her love confession came to mind. If that wasn't feelings aligning, she didn't know what was. "So we're bonded now because of Resonate?"

"More than that, my dear. Teaghan can use your powers."

Teaghan startled. "Say what now?"

Niccolo gestured between them. "You can touch her necromes without it hurting, correct?"

"Yeah, but it's been that way since she cast Recognize."

"True. How about another test?" Niccolo nodded to one of his Renfields.

The man on his left said, "Activate."

The muffled hum of a powerful necrome sounded beneath the sleeve of his jacket. Jeliyah marveled at how easily she could pinpoint the necrome's location. It was an upper-arm cuff. Most male necromancers favored that design or bracers since they were easy to wear under clothing.

Niccolo asked, "Well?"

Teaghan shrugged. "Well, what?"

"How do you feel?"

"Don't know what you're talking about."

Niccolo chuckled with a shake of his head. "Think about it a few seconds. I'm sure you'll figure it out."

Jeliyah didn't know what Niccolo was hinting at, so she

couldn't offer Teaghan a suggestion to soothe his growing annoyance at Niccolo's cryptic behavior. The humming filled the silence while they waited. Jeliyah listened to the melody, appreciating being able to hear a necrome she wasn't wearing. It made her medallion and rings vibrate, as though they were asking to be activated too.

"Do it," Teaghan said.

She looked at him in surprise and then turned her gaze to Niccolo, who made an offering gesture. She shrugged. "Activate."

Her necromes hummed to life along with those of the second Renfield. He clutched his waist—a belt-buckle necrome.

Niccolo clapped. "Brava, Jeliyah. Beautifully done. You confirmed my next question without my asking."

"Question?"

"Deactivate."

All necromes silenced, and it was Jeliyah's turn to be confused. "What? But I didn't."

"No, you didn't. It is the mark of a truly powerful necromancer to use necromes not in their possession. Only a precious rhodium level can do it. I wasn't able until after I donned vampirism. It would seem your bond with Teaghan puts you almost equal in power to me."

Hearing that didn't make Jeliyah happy. The last thing she needed was Niccolo seeing her as a threat.

He said, "You will need to learn to focus your commands unless your intention is to use all necromes in your vicinity. You can cast some interesting spells that way, but I wouldn't suggest making a habit of it unless you want to make yourself a target."

Was that a threat? Niccolo didn't act threatening, but Jeliyah had learned to rely on her instincts and the little intuitions that warned of danger. She nodded. "I'll try to remember that."

"Good girl."

Teaghan said, "My skin didn't crawl."

Niccolo clapped again. "And the light bulb goes off."

"I don't understand," Jeliyah said.

"The crawling sensation vampires complain about when in the presence of necromes is the magic of their body being negated. Teaghan is no longer suffering from that particular malady thanks to your bond giving him access to your necromancer abilities. The magic keeping him alive has changed and become more resilient.

"From my understanding, the exchange goes both ways. It would have been a mutual exchange if you hadn't been changed. You would have had access to Teaghan's vampiric abilities and immortality while he had access to your necromancer powers. Something similar to a Renfield connection without the forced servitude. It's my belief that Renfields came about to mimic Resonate after the spell was banned and purposefully forgotten. However, you are your own vampire, so now only Teaghan benefits from the exchange."

This was too much. Recognize. Resonate. The blood sharing. The sex. All of it was her fault because she'd misread a book and dabbled with spells she didn't fully comprehend. It was over and done with now, but her eagerness to prove she had worth beyond her womb had led her on a reckless path.

What's worse, she had dragged Teaghan along with her. She'd kept blaming him for making her move at his pace, when she'd been the one to set it. Prior connection or not, she shouldn't be tied to Teaghan.

"I have a task for you two." Niccolo walked back around his desk and sat. "I find the little coup in the next territory to be a trifle annoying. I lost a good man over it already."

"You lost?" Teaghan pointed at him. "That rogue belonged to you?"

"Yes, the rogue you killed belonged to me. I sent him only because Fredrick promised his protection. I demanded the heads of the enforcers who failed that duty."

"What about me?"

"Well, that is a conundrum, isn't it? Imagine my surprise when the vampire I ordered Fredrick to dispose of for killing my man is the very same one seeking asylum from me through one of my most trusted. His sire, even. I decided to meet you."

"And?"

"You're an enforcer. Nothing more, nothing less. You were doing a job, hunting a rogue who should have never been given rogue status. I blame Fredrick for that, not you. He concocted that asinine plan, citing some bullshit about plausible deniability and such should my messenger be caught. I should have seen the situation for what it was."

Jeliyah asked, "What does that mean?"

"It means Fredrick is working both sides. Or that's how I see it. He could have gotten an invitation for my messenger rather than trying to send nonaggressive enforcers to a fake rogue hunt. But Fredrick doesn't want to get his hands dirty. He wants to look innocent in case the coup doesn't happen and the usurper betrays him. He can use the dead messenger as proof he was acting in the best interests of the Marceaux family the entire time."

Teaghan grumbled, "I should have shot him in the head when he pulled me off that hunt."

Niccolo frowned. "Did Fredrick give you the hunt?"

"No, I called dispatch. I'd been hounding them for a hunt. When I called, the manager gave me the first name on the list to get me off his back. Fredrick met me on site and cited the no-partner, no-hunt rule before carting me off to meet Jeliyah. The twins were there when we resumed the hunt."

Jeliyah said, "He went back to the hunt without telling anyone." Teaghan glared at her and she snapped, "What? You did. If you had called dispatch, they probably would have told you they gave the hunt to the twins and to take the night off."

"And you wouldn't be a vampire tied to me now. Is that what you're saying?" Teaghan ground out.

"I didn't say that."

"You're thinking it, sweetness. You didn't have to say it."

"Teaghan—"

Niccolo shushed them with a finger to his lips. "You two can settle that argument on the way back to kill Fredrick for me."

Teaghan asked, "How much?"

"Double your usual fee for both of you. I hate double-dealing. I've rescinded my aid to the usurper. His offer to me isn't worth this headache. I now plan to relieve him of a traitor as a parting gift."

"Done." Teaghan stood and left the room.

Jeliyah stared after him, not needing access to his thoughts to know he was pissed. She faced Niccolo and asked, "Does Resonate come with a telepathic connection?"

"Indeed, it does."

She sighed.

"There are ways to block the connection. Even the closest couple needs time apart every now and again."

She agreed.

Teaghan shouldn't have heard that thought. Or rather, he shouldn't have interpreted it the way he had. She wasn't his type. Mekhail had said so, and she'd seen it for herself. Teaghan should be pissed Jeliyah's ineptitude had saddled him with a woman he didn't want.

She rose from her seat. "I have to get ready."

"One more thing, my dear." Niccolo stood. "You are a vampire now, but you are still a necromancer. Most will see you as a necromancer before a vampire. The secret that the two can blend is a well-kept one. Vampires will doubt their senses that you are one of them. Use that to your advantage."

"Thank you."

"Of course. I help my own. You are one of mine now. Know that your debts will be gone by the time you return."

"Thank you again." Jeliyah nodded to him and left the room, headed for Teaghan. She didn't know how to fix this new rift between them or if she should. Spiritual connection or not,

Resonate or not, Teaghan didn't fit her image of the man she would have chosen for herself.

By the time she arrived at the room, Teaghan had already changed to his normal gangsta attire. He was shirtless and strapping his sword in place when she entered. The way he turned his back on her spoke volumes. It was also childish.

Five days ago she was riding a desk, dreaming of retirement. Yesterday, she was mortal. Her entire world had been flipped because of some vampire's machinations to seize power.

As she'd said to Niccolo, she didn't waste time speculating on the past and how the present would be changed if things had been different. There was no point. Time travel didn't exist. This was her life now. Tied to a man who could dance around inside her mind at his leisure—misinterpreting her thoughts and judging her —without ever sharing any of himself.

Teaghan swung around and glared at her.

"People who eavesdrop hear nothing good about themselves." She walked past him to a new pile of clothes she assumed were for her. She stripped off her dress and changed into the jeans and button-up cotton shirt, happy for normal clothes at last.

Someone knocked at the door. Teaghan didn't acknowledge it, so Jeliyah said, "Come in."

Mekhail opened the door and entered. "I come bearing gifts from Niccolo to help with your hunt." He held out a palm-sized flat box to Jeliyah. "For you, miss."

She knew what it was without having to open the box—necro-metal. Powerful necro-metal from the way it hummed without a necromancer's will behind it. She undid the ribbon and opened the box, revealing an ornate locket.

Mekhail said, "Niccolo wished you to have this. He said it belonged to his sister. It is made from her blood."

Jeliyah touched the locket with hesitant fingers. "It's gorgeous." She lifted the necro-metal chain so the locket dangled before her eyes. "Tell him thank you for me."

"Of course, miss."

She opened the locket, expecting to find a picture, but it was empty. Whatever treasure the locket held when in its previous owner's possession had probably been removed when the woman passed.

Jeliyah yanked her medallion from her neck, not caring if she broke the chain since it was cheap. The medallion fit snugly inside the locket, which she closed, and then hung around her neck. Both the locket and medallion hummed together, complementing each other in a melody only a necromancer could appreciate. The sound soothed her nerves.

Mekhail pulled a ring box from his pocket and said to Teaghan, "Niccolo also gives you a gift, sire. He says now that you have access to necromancer abilities, you will need the means to use them. These also belonged to his sister, but he reasons a man with your fashion sense won't let that deter him."

Teaghan snatched up the box and opened it. He smirked, grabbed the contents in a fist, and tossed the box back to Mekhail. Then he did something to the upper part of his left ear.

Jeliyah couldn't tell what he was doing until he moved his hands. Two stud earrings, each with a diamond chip in the center, sat side by side on the edge of his ear.

Necromancers of old, before humans found out vampires were real, had to wear their weapons in plain sight. Necro-metal in those days had taken on the guise of jewelry and other everyday items—cuff links, fob watches, even glasses. One necromancer was said to have made an entire saddle and bridle for his horse from necro-metal. The archive of Jeliyah's former campus housed the tiara a necromancer from an old royal family had worn.

Teaghan said, "Let's do this."

Jeliyah nodded, ready to have the task finished so she could come back and hide in a dark corner until she figured out the new course of her life.

Mekhail held out a set of keys. "Your car is fueled and waiting."

Teaghan took them on his way out of the room.

Jeliyah followed him but had to pause when Mekhail grabbed her hand. She looked at the man in question.

He smiled sadly. "My sire is an awkward man, though he doesn't seem it, miss. He can kill. He can fuck. He knows nothing of love. Give him time."

"You're in luck, since time seems to be the one thing I have in abundance all of a sudden." She patted his hand, finding that his words soothed her hurt feelings. "Thank you, and I'll keep your words in mind."

"Happy hunting, miss." He laid a kiss on her knuckles before releasing her.

Jeliyah, who always seemed to be trailing after Teaghan, met him at the car. *His* car. She stared at it in surprise, much the same way he was. She asked, "Is that really your car?"

He nodded.

"How?"

"Looks like Niccolo had someone bring it back, and they fixed it overnight." He caressed the driver-side door, the one that had bullet holes the day before. "They did a good job."

"Looks like you don't have to waste money getting it fixed after all." She walked around the car and got in the passenger seat. "Let's go. There's a dead man standing between me and some much-needed rest."

Teaghan hopped the door in his usual fashion. "Speaking of, go down. You need to get used to shutting down at set intervals and how it feels."

If Jeliyah's heart still beat according to her emotions and not as a simple function to move her blood, it would be pounding right about now. Vampire sleep was allowing herself to die.

"It's not dying. The humans think that because we've got no heartbeat. Just close your eyes. You did it last night without worrying about it as much as you are now."

That was right, she had gone to sleep last night after her

change. It hadn't occurred to her to be scared. She'd been too tired. She decided to trust Teaghan and closed her eyes.

She tried to relax. This was part of her life now. She had to sleep or else she would age and then deteriorate.

Teaghan started the car and peeled out of the drive.

Jeliyah slapped her hands over her ears with a cry of pain. The squealing tires could have been hundreds of nails scratching a chalkboard through a football stadium sound system and she wouldn't have known the difference.

"Sorry about that." He opened the glove box and pulled out a pair of his earplugs. "Wear these for the next few days. It'll help with the adjustment. Use the shades too."

"What about you?" She stuffed the earplugs in and jammed the shades in place. It was night and yet the headlights and street lamps shined like tiny suns. How could Teaghan stand it?

"I've been like this for a while, sweetness. I've adapted. You will too. Until then, shades and earplugs. We might have to get you some gloves too."

"Remind me why I wanted this again," she grumbled under her breath.

She didn't think she would need the gloves. Her skin was more sensitive. She could feel every fiber of the clothing she wore, as if they were separate pieces of thick yarn. The reasoning behind the vampire preference for silks and satins—and little-to-no clothing or very loose clothing in Teaghan's case—now made sense. But her skin was acclimating faster than her other senses, possibly because there was no way to dampen what her skin encountered.

"Stop complaining and sleep already," Teaghan said.

She wished she had thicker earplugs or a better brand, but made do with what she had. Jeliyah closed her eyes again.

Teaghan had reached the highway before she got herself calm enough to let the sleep pull her under. It wasn't like human sleeping, but then she'd known that already. Her mind remained active, along with her other senses. She heard every car that passed and the hum of the car engine vibrated through her.

Her temperature dropped to match her surroundings. The sensation of her consciousness curling into a comfortable ball while the rest of her body remained upright on her seat intrigued her. It was almost as if her mind had separated itself.

{*Not so bad, right?*} Teaghan asked through their mental link.

{*Doesn't talking like this disturb my rest?*}

{*Nope. The mind and body separating is vampiric sleeping. The mind staying with the body too long taxes the body until the deterioration starts. Only blood and lots of it can fix the damage. When there is nothing left, the mind shuts down, and the body takes control to hunt for food.*}

{*And that's why crazed vampires attack anyone with a pulse.*} More revelations. The speculation of her former teachers had only scratched the surface of what the vampires truly endured.

Sleep wasn't just the need to remain human-looking. It also kept vampires from becoming mindless killing machines. Jeliyah imagined that losing one's consciousness to the frenzied need to feed had to feel horrible.

"It does," Teaghan whispered.

For the first time since seeing the jagged, sunken scar that ran across his chest, Jeliyah got another insight into Teaghan's life before she met him. If they were going to be stuck with each other, he would need to share a lot more or else this relationship wouldn't work.

"Do you want it to work, necromancer?"

Jeliyah turned her mind to soaring eagles and windswept mountains to keep from answering a question she didn't have an answer for yet.

CHAPTER

ELEVEN

Jeliyah entered the hotel room, a little surprised their stuff was still there and unmolested after three days. The staff must have assumed she and Teaghan were still there. That meant she didn't have to buy new clothes just yet. She hadn't wanted to waste time worrying about wardrobe while back on her old stomping grounds.

The second they'd entered the city, Jeliyah had felt as if people were walking over her grave. She'd looked over her shoulder every other second when she visited the bank to retrieve the contents of her safe-deposit box, hoping Niccolo's words held true and people would see her as a necromancer before sensing her as a vampire.

So long as she stayed close to Teaghan, they would think the vampire alert originated from him and not her. She didn't want her former acquaintances trying to hunt and kill her—the only punishment for a necromancer turned vampire.

Teaghan said into his phone, "You'll find us in the same spot where I killed the twins' rogue. Be there." He stabbed the call end button and holstered his phone. "We're on. You ready?"

Jeliyah looked around the room, wishing she could stay there and pretend to be her version of human again—a naïve necromancer only concerned with retirement. She nodded as she shouldered her duffel bag with ease, almost throwing it across the room because she put too much strength into picking it up. Instead of a duffel bag full of clothes and other personal items, it more felt like it was full of freshly spun cotton candy. In other words, her new strength made it feel as if it weighed next to nothing.

She said, "Let's get it done."

Grabbing his own bag, Teaghan led the way back to the car, where they stashed their things in the trunk. He made quick work of checking out and then drove them to the meeting spot.

After parking the car, Teaghan said, "Lose the shades and pull your hair over your ears."

Jeliyah didn't question it. She had to play human. Doing it while at the bank had nearly blinded her. LED lighting should be considered a hate crime against vampires.

She'd excused her reaction to the people who noticed her wincing as a piercing migraine, which hadn't been far off the truth since a splitting headache had hit her the moments the lights had, climbing in intensity the longer she stayed. As with most things where vampires were concerned, the pain subsided the moment she left the bank. She still didn't want to go through it again.

The grounds surrounding the Marceaux estate were vampire friendly and blessedly dark. Jeliyah's vampire eyes saw every detail of the roots and trees around her as though they were bathed in light.

What she thought would be a cacophony of noise from night creatures sounded no different to her vampire ears than to her former human ones. While louder than before, the ambient noise could be ignored, so it didn't bother her.

What she couldn't tune out was the heat Teaghan radiated across the short distance that separated them. Vampires gave off heat just the same as any other warm-blooded animal. All part of the mind inhabiting the body. And Teaghan's body inhabited every part of her mind.

His scent of musk was the only one she smelled. His heat turned the cool night into a hot summer's day. She didn't understand this reaction. She'd sat beside him in the car for almost twenty-four hours without a single errant thought. He'd slept for a few hours at a rest stop before continuing to the hotel without her thoughts turning to sex. A few minutes in the open forest and suddenly her libido revved to life.

She faced the tree she stood near and focused on memorizing the pattern of the bark. The jagged pattern reminded her of Teaghan's scarred chest and how the rough skin felt when she licked it. The memory made her pussy tingle with need.

A surprised gasp ripped from her throat when Teaghan crowded her close to the tree.

"Quiet," he snapped in a harsh whisper.

He must have heard something she missed while she'd occupied herself musing about sex. Her errant thoughts would get her killed. She needed to focus.

Or that was her plan until Teaghan undid her jeans and yanked them down her legs. She tried to pull away from him, but he held her trapped with his arms on either side of her.

She asked, "What are you doing?"

"Getting you off so you stop distracting me."

"You—" Her words ended on a sharp cry of pleasure as Teaghan surged his hard dick into the depths of her pussy.

She clawed at the tree, shredding the bark, and whimpered loudly. Her whole body tightened as an instant orgasm claimed her. No warning or buildup—the sensation of Teaghan buried inside her hurtled her over the edge of ecstasy. She squeezed her eyes shut and sucked at her bottom lip.

"We're just getting started, sweetness." He pulled back and then thrust home again.

The remnants of the last orgasm combined with the next and

had Jeliyah panting and crying. It was too much. The sweet sensation far surpassed the night before last.

"You were new then, still changing." He pressed his hips against her ass, shifting his erection inside her and prolonging her overexcited state. "What you're feeling isn't an orgasm, sweetness. You have to readjust your scale. This is just titillation." He kissed her hair. "When you orgasm, the whole forest will know it."

Grabbing her in a firm grip, Teaghan pumped in a fast tempo that left Jeliyah breathless and happy she didn't need air, because she couldn't pull it in fast enough. Despite the overwhelming assault to her new senses, she found herself pushing back against Teaghan and circling her hips so she impaled herself on his length.

Teaghan hugged her waist with one arm as he moved with her. His breath came out in huffs that feathered across her neck. He kissed her there, scraping his fangs over her skin.

Her keen of need filled the night. She wanted his fangs. It surprised her how much she wanted them. Some part of her knew his bite would feel as good as his dick.

Teaghan nibbled at her neck, teasing her. "Beg." He punctuated his command by flicking her clit.

Jeliyah's eyes rolled skyward, and she arched back so her head rested on Teaghan's shoulder and the rough bark of the tree excited her nipples through her shirt. As much as she wanted to heed Teaghan's command, her mouth wouldn't obey her. All she could manage were sounds to convey the unmatched pleasure he was giving her. She didn't know if she could handle the vampire version of an orgasm if her current state was the preamble.

"Aren't you two cozy? And vulnerable." The newcomer's words barely registered before Teaghan snatched Jeliyah's gun from its holster and shoved it against the forehead of the man who'd spoken.

Teaghan snapped, "Fuck off." At the same time, he pulled the trigger.

The man didn't have time to dodge. His head snapped back as

the bullet entered, killing him as it blew out the back of his head. The death and smell of blood sobered Jeliyah a little.

She stared at the corpse. "Who was that?"

"Who the fuck cares? Shut up and come." He pinched her clit and increased the tempo of his thrusts.

Jeliyah had no choice but to let the pleasure suck her under once more. If she'd been human, the gruesome scene would have killed her libido. Her vampire self had no such issues. The scent of blood excited her and made her fangs lengthen.

She shoved back, dislodging Teaghan, and turned. With a small kick, she freed one foot from her pants so she could wrap her legs around Teaghan's waist. The force of her jumping on him backed him up against another tree.

He laughed as he cupped her ass, squeezing it and guiding her pussy onto his shaft. "That's right, sweetness. Fuck that dick."

An animalistic rumble of satisfaction left her throat as she bounced, driving Teaghan's erection deep so his tip teased her core. She let her head fall back, secure in the knowledge that Teaghan would protect her so she could let the passion of the moment sweep her away.

Teaghan ripped her shirt open and latched his mouth on to her left nipple. He sucked it and thrilled it with his tongue, not letting up until she cried out loud enough that a few night birds took flight to escape the sound. When he switched nipples, he dragged his mouth over her skin between her breasts.

Her other nipple got a few licks before Teaghan bit her, sinking his fangs into the swell of her breast. Crackling white noise filled her mind and made her skin tingle. Her movements stopped as she convulsed. Teaghan had been right. Everything until that point had been preliminary. The marvelous gratification rendered her incapable of doing anything except reveling in it.

Vampires should have invented a new word for this sensation long ago, because orgasm wasn't potent enough. Climax, zenith, pinnacle—no word equaled the strength of something this glorious. A strength that built when Teaghan squeezed her ass and guided her to keep riding, to continue bringing them both to gratification.

Jeliyah didn't think it possible to experience another soul-searing orgasm so soon after the first, but her body proved her wrong. It craved everything Teaghan had to give and demanded more. She let the abyss have her and found herself enveloped in a warm glow that she craved more than the heat. The glow soothed her frenzied emotions, allowing a sense of peace and rightness to settle around her.

Some intuition told her Teaghan felt it too. He released his bite and hugged her waist. His head rested between her breasts as he shook from his own release. He was breathing hard. That simple fact made Jeliyah smile.

Teaghan had had centuries to acclimate to his vampire body, but Jeliyah still had the ability to leave him panting. He growled under his breath, but didn't correct her thoughts. She hugged his shoulders, basking in the glow they shared.

She didn't know how long they stayed that way before Teaghan lifted his head and met her gaze. He searched her face with an expression of uncertainty marring his features. It didn't look right on him.

He whispered, "I'm sorry."

Jeliyah gave him a sad smile as she cupped his face and laid her lips against his. The kiss they shared was gentle and conveyed more than thoughts and words ever could. The bond Jeliyah had forged was permanent. They were part of each other. Once they finished this hunt, maybe they could finally find a quiet place to talk so they could find out what that truly meant.

Teaghan nodded. He kissed her lips once more before lifting her up so she released his dick—an action that had her libido readying for the next round. She tamped down the urge that made her want to hop back on and ride toward another explosive encounter. This wasn't the time or the place.

"Later," Teaghan whispered against her neck. He set her on her feet.

While she expected to be wobbly, Jeliyah found her vampire body recovered faster than her mind. Her stance was solid without Teaghan's help, though he kept hold of her waist until she stepped away. Her pants dragged the ground.

The sight of her pants dangling from one leg—the jeans still hugged her left calf, though partially inside out—made her chuckle. Even more amusing was that she had to take off her right shoe to get the pant leg back on when she hadn't needed it off to get the pant leg off.

Teaghan made a sound of appreciation before grabbing her ass.

Jeliyah squeaked and straightened quickly from her bent position. She smacked Teaghan's hand to get him to let go.

He said, "No panties. It's always the quiet ones into the freaky shit."

Jeliyah yanked up her jeans and did up the zipper and button. "I am not. Niccolo didn't supply any with the clothes he gave me."

"You's a freak." Teaghan laughed when she swatted at him. "Don't get mad at me because you like going commando and getting a piece in the woods."

"It takes two to tango, vampire."

"I never said I wasn't a freak. Any time, any place, is good for me. Say when."

Jeliyah opened her mouth to give him a flippant reply when a second intruder said, "When."

Jeliyah and Teaghan turned toward Fredrick, who stood a few feet away with four others flanking him. One of the four was Ephraim, the vampire who had chatted with Jeliyah in the club the other night.

Fredrick gestured at the corpse of the man Teaghan had killed earlier. "Considering what you did to my associate, I thought it best to let you two finish before making my presence known. I wouldn't want to end up the same way."

Teaghan asked, "Enjoy the show?"

"It was invigorating. I'm happy you brought her back, Teaghan. The others are now eager to partake of the sample you gave us." Fredrick licked his lips as he admired Jeliyah's bared breasts. "I admit to my own eagerness. I've heard necromancers can be quite stimulating."

Jeliyah didn't bother acting embarrassed or trying to pull her shirt closed—some buttons were gone and some of the button loops torn thanks to Teaghan. Let Fredrick and his friends look. If any of the men touched her, they would fry. Her necromes buzzed as they turned active without her voicing the command.

Her personal shield snapped into place, lighting up the night with its blue glow. She said, "I'm more than stimulating, vampire. I'm electric. I'll be happy to give you a taste if you want it that badly." She held out her hand to him.

Fredrick tsked at her and wagged his finger. "Give me more credit than that, necromancer. When I claim you, it will be after an open invitation. I understand the trustees have a way to compel you to give the invitation, whether you want to or not."

"They'll never get the chance." Not to mention she was a vampire, so the invitation caveat no longer applied to her.

But she didn't say that last part since it didn't seem as if Fredrick had realized she was no longer one of the living. Niccolo had been right. So long as she didn't exhibit any vampiric traits and kept her hair over her earplugs, Fredrick and his friends would keep underestimating her as a simple necromancer.

Teaghan said, "Enough. I've got a message for you from Niccolo, Fredrick."

"The message is clear. He's sent you back to face your doom, as I knew he would. You were a fool to run straight into the arms of the man who ordered your execution."

"And you're an idiot if you think Niccolo is the type of man who would let me drive twenty-some odd hours to be killed when he has two necromancers at his beck and call who could have done the deed right then and there."

Fredrick's smile faltered.

Teaghan nodded. "That's right, Fredrick. I didn't escape. He sent me back on assignment. I've got a sizable bounty waiting for me when I bring him your head." He pulled his sword. "Time's a wasting."

"Kill them both!" Fredrick bellowed that command, pointing at them.

The rush of ten extra men from the trees surprised Jeliyah. She'd been too focused on the few in front of her to realize Fredrick had her and Teaghan surrounded.

Had Teaghan known?

{Yup, I did. Beat yourself up later, necromancer. Kick ass now.} Teaghan rushed forward with a battle cry. Three of the men, Ephraim amongst them, raced to intercept him.

Jeliyah stared on in confusion, unsure of what to do. The crackling of her personal shield intensified as the vampires closed in on her.

Fredrick said, "That shield won't last forever, necromancer. You're wasting energy needlessly. Just give in."

She started to retort as a way of bluffing him into thinking she would last longer than he predicted, but stopped herself. Taking a mental tally of herself revealed the shield wasn't depleting her. She felt fine. More than that, she felt strong.

The platinum level necrome nestled between her breasts hummed loudly, as though happy to be in use once more. It channeled her power with little effort. No wonder platinum level necromes cost so much.

Whether she had platinum level necromes or not, she didn't know her limits. The change from human to vampire had been too sudden for her to test herself. She hadn't tasted blood yet either. She didn't want to do too much and end up passing out, leaving Teaghan to protect them both. Did vampires pass out?

{No, necromancer! Now kill some of these fuckers before I turn you over my knee and beat your ass.}

Her pussy twitched, sending a shiver up her spine. *{That sounds fun.}*

{Oh, you little slut. I've got something for you later. Just wait.}

Jeliyah laughed and sent Teaghan a mental air kiss.

Fredrick said, "I'm glad to amuse you."

"You do, Fredrick. You really do." She pointed to the man closest to her. "Break."

The man exploded, raining chunks and blood over the group. The shield kept any from touching her.

She laughed more. "That was even more amusing. Let's do it again." She pointed at another man but he blurred out of view, charging her before she could speak.

He must have thought his vampiric speed could save him. He had another think coming. Jeliyah could see him.

The man darted behind a tree before rushing her, probably to ram her shield and force her to slam against the tree behind her, knocking her out. It wouldn't work. She let him get close before she said, "Halt."

The man froze mid-step with a look of surprise. He tried to say something as she pulled in a loud breath before saying, "Break."

Like the man before him, he exploded in chunks and blood.

Fredrick stumbled back to avoid being splattered. His expression was one of disbelief. "What... How... You're a palladium level. Casting one Break should have taken most of your strength."

"Shoulda, woulda, coulda," she said with a shrug before casting Break on another vampire who had started to edge away from the group, probably trying to escape.

To Teaghan, she said, *{It's time to stop playing, lover.}*

{Mmmm... I like the sound of that. Say it again.}

Jeliyah was confused for a second before she smiled and said in a purring mental voice, *{Lover.}*

{Damn. I like that.} Teaghan let out a man purr with a big grin on his face. *{Tell me what to do.}*

She opened her mind to Teaghan, letting him have access to years of necromancer training. It was time for Fredrick to find out just how bad his situation was. She and Teaghan would give him a few minutes to regret his life choices before taking his head.

Teaghan rifled through the information Jeliyah showed him, looking for something he could use immediately. Break was too messy and not his style. He wanted to do some personal damage to the men clashing swords with him. Something that would hurt... a lot.

He grinned as he found just the right spell. "Activate," he growled.

The necro-metal earrings sang a familiar melody in his ear. He hummed along with them, confusing his opponents. The men faltered in their attack, looking between Teaghan and Jeliyah to discern the trick. They would never figure it out.

Teaghan closed a mental hand around the power Jeliyah had given him and said, "Cleanse."

He pointed the attack at Ephraim first as payback for that stunt in the club.

The man burst into blue flames while the others jumped back in surprise. But they weren't fast enough and couldn't escape when Teaghan directed the flames to engulf them as well. All three screamed as the fire melted flesh from bone. It wouldn't kill them or end their agony until every bit of flesh had been burned away. The magic that animated vampires was cruel like that.

Teaghan wasn't that patient, though. He severed the men's heads from their necks and left their corpses to burn to ash.

Fredrick screamed, "What is this?! How are you doing this?! What are you?!"

The other attackers all stopped advancing. The scent of fear filled the air. Two men started backing into the shadows.

Teaghan said, "Jeliyah, don't let them leave."

"On it." She raised her arms. "Enclose." Her personal shield dropped so it could reform around the group.

A scream filled the air as one man tried the barrier and died for his trouble, electrocuted until he exploded. The others stared at Jeliyah in open horror. Fredrick was among that number.

She said, "You've seen our little surprise. We can't let any of you leave here alive. In your next life, choose your friends better."

Fredrick pulled a gun and fired, hitting Jeliyah in the chest. She went down with a scream of pain and Teaghan bellowing her name.

Teaghan ran to her side, dropping his sword so he could cradle her in his arms.

"I don't like guns, but we use the tools available to us," Fredrick said as he pointed the gun at Teaghan. "Goodbye, Teaghan. You can join your little necromancer bitch in hell."

Teaghan laughed. He dropped his forehead to rest against Jeliyah's and indulged his relieved amusement. Jeliyah wasn't dying.

Fredrick had hit her heart, but the bond she shared with Teaghan kept her alive. Teaghan could feel his life sustaining hers, keeping her with him while she healed the vampire equivalent of a fatal wound. She would live.

"What's so fucking funny, you bastard?"

"You haven't noticed something very important, Fredrick." Teaghan raised his head and met Fredrick's gaze.

"What?"

"Look around." Teaghan waited as Fredrick did a quick glance about.

The others did the same before bringing their gazes back to Teaghan. He could almost see the ripple of realization as each man figured out the problem.

Fredrick was the slowest to connect the dots. His gun pointed at the ground as his grip went slack and his jaw dropped open. "How? I shot her. I killed her!"

Teaghan glanced up at the still-crackling barrier that would keep everyone inside until Jeliyah lowered it. Actually, until Teaghan lowered it. Jeliyah had given him control of the spell so she could focus on healing.

He laid a kiss on her forehead before lowering her to the ground and standing up straight. Confronting Fredrick, he said, "She said it already. You've seen our surprise. You can't leave here alive."

"Fuck you!" Fredrick tightened his grip on the gun and fired.

Teaghan sidestepped and the bullet passed him without damage. "There's a reason vampires don't use guns, Fredrick. You know that. You want me dead, you'll have to man up and do it the hard way." He glanced at his discarded sword. He could get it if he left Jeliyah's side, but that wasn't going to happen. He sighed and shook his head. "I'm done playing with you, Fredrick."

"You—"

"Sever."

A slice of wind passed through Fredrick's neck. The man's shocked expression would remain frozen in place until his head was destroyed.

Teaghan knelt beside Jeliyah again. Her chest wound had closed, but they were both weakening from the repair job. He glanced at the vampires awaiting his next move. He gave them props for not pleading for their lives like cowards. They were all enforcers—without their necromancers, no less. Whoever had been giving Fredrick orders must have wanted the trustees kept out the loop. That meant leaving the necromancers at home. Like Ephraim had done the night he introduced himself to Jeliyah.

Since Teaghan didn't know the men, that meant they weren't high enough in the ranks to be missed.

He tried one last spell and hoped it worked the way he wanted with the energy he had left. "Frozen."

The remaining men all jolted as the spell held them bound.

Teaghan felt the barrier weakening. He had to act fast. He ran to the closest man, bared his neck, and bit him.

Teaghan drained the man, feeding for himself and Jeliyah. The sustenance made the barrier sizzle to renewed life. Teaghan went to his next victim. By the time he finished draining the second man, Jeliyah was off the ground and feeding on one of the others. She picked up the technique from his thoughts.

Teaghan smiled and stood back to watch. He would need to stop her so she didn't get drunk. It was a human misconception that vampires could only feed on human blood. Blood was blood. Human was more potent than most animals, and vampire blood was easier to assimilate. Vampires didn't feed off one another as a courtesy. Besides, human blood tasted better.

Jeliyah made a disgusted noise. "I hope so. This is nasty. If I wasn't so hungry, I wouldn't have drunk as much as I had."

Teaghan jerked his chin to one of the last four men standing. "Do one more before we kill the rest and get out of here."

She looked around at the bodies strewn about. "What about cleanup?"

"Not my problem. Feed."

Teaghan heard her mind balking as she bit the next man. He didn't enjoy seeing her lips touching another. Only the knowledge that she needed blood kept Teaghan from pulling her away.

She finished with another disgusted noise. The vampire she'd drunk dry, killing him, dropped to the ground when she released him. She said, "Break."

The last three men exploded.

Teaghan watched the phenomenon with morbid interest. He preferred Cleanse, but he also preferred death. Jeliyah was the type who wanted it quick, if not clean. Break provided that.

He lowered the barrier and then stopped short. Their little light show had gathered an audience. He moved to shield Jeliyah from the group of vampires surrounding the perimeter of the barrier.

A woman walked through the crowd, which parted for her. Lanore, head of the Marceaux family. She looked around at the carnage before leveling her gaze on Teaghan. "Why have you done this, enforcer?"

"They got in the way of my bounty and tried to kill my necromancer."

"Who is your bounty?"

"Fredrick."

Lanore frowned. "He is a member of the reserve, not a rogue."

"He's a traitor, and Niccolo put a price on his head."

"Niccolo?" She looked thoughtful. "Do you belong to him now, enforcer? Is that what you're saying?"

"I'm saying I got stabbed in the back for doing my job. Since Fredrick did the stabbing, I took the job to collect his head. Simple as that."

"And if I take offense at you accepting a bounty from an outside family while in my territory, in my front yard?"

"You can if you want, but I did you a favor. Fredrick was helping a usurper to your power."

"Do you have proof of this, or merely Niccolo's word?"

"What I've got is a whole lot of don't give a shit. You can play indignant and oblivious if you want. Let me know how that works out for you when the one gunning for your ass gets the balls to do it in the open."

Jeliyah fisted her hands in the back of his shirt. Her anxiety at his irreverent attitude played through his mind. He couldn't do anything to calm or reassure her. Either they were leaving, or they were dead. No matter the outcome, he wasn't kowtowing to some wannabe royal bitch who probably hadn't stepped out of her house in decades.

Lanore regarded him for a long while. She narrowed her eyes before heaving a sigh and waving.

The vampires dispersed a few at a time until only five remained standing behind her.

She said, "Take Fredrick's head back to Niccolo and never return to my territory, enforcer. If you do, I will have you hunted as a rogue."

"Fine by me." Teaghan kept Jeliyah close as he walked over to Fredrick's head.

"Leave the girl."

"Fuck you."

"You will watch—"

"I repeat. Fuck you. She's with me, and I'm with Niccolo. You don't like it, take it up with him."

"You haven't left my territory yet, enforcer."

"Oh, I'm sick of this shit. Jeliyah, if you please." He glanced over his shoulder at her.

She startled with wide eyes and then looked at Lanore. With a shrug, Jeliyah said, "Ghosting."

The sentries tightened around Lanore and pulled their swords.

Teaghan didn't know why. "Ghosting?"

"Like Ghost Status, but it makes us invisible, not just the marker. Grab the head. This takes a bigger toll than Ghost Status, and I've never cast it before, so I don't know how long I can hold it."

"Right." He balled his fingers in Fredrick's hair and, with his free hand, pulled her along behind him back to the car. The sounds of pursuit soon reached him.

For the first time since meeting her, Teaghan watched Jeliyah jump into the car, not bothering with the door. She said, "Good thing we did all our errands before this. Let's get the hell out of here."

"Don't gotta tell me twice." Teaghan passed her Fredrick's head, jumped in the car, and screeched out of the parking lot at top speed. He didn't know if Lanore would continue the pursuit after they left her estate, and had no plans to stop outside the front gate to find out.

He tossed his phone on the dash after hitting the speed dial. The phone rang twice before Mekhail picked up. "Hello, sire."

"We've got the head and trouble. Tell Niccolo to call in a favor or something, or you might have a war."

"Of course, sire. I shall call back with news." The line went silent.

Teaghan glanced at Jeliyah. "How you doing?"

"I've felt better, which isn't saying much since I've only been a vampire for a short time."

"Deactivate and go down. If trouble hits, I'll wake you."

"Okay." She looked at the head she held. "Before that, do you have a bag for this?"

He gestured to the glove box.

Jeliyah pulled out a plastic bag, stuffed Fredrick's head in it and then dropped it on the floor between her feet. She heaved a tired sigh that Teaghan wanted to echo. He was too busy straining his senses for sounds of an imminent attack.

All he heard was the empty night, which had him glancing at Jeliyah every few seconds to make sure she was still there.

Her lack of heartbeat shouldn't scare him as much as it did, but he couldn't forget the hole she'd had in her chest minutes before and how he'd thought he'd lost her. He never wanted to feel that again. That meant hearing an attack before it hit.

The phone almost deafened him when it rang. He stabbed the talk button. "Tell me good news."

"Of course, sire. Niccolo has contacted the Marceaux matron and explained the situation to her. She is angered at your disrespect but has called off the hunt for your head. You can return at your leisure."

"We're headed back now. Have food waiting for us. Jeliyah will need it."

"We await your return, sire."

Teaghan ended the call and let himself sag. Things had gotten deeper than he'd liked. At least they came out of it alive. He glanced at Jeliyah. In a few hours, they were going to have a long talk. He wanted all the cards on the table. He knew she wanted the same.

At the end of the talk, they would know if what had passed between them in the woods was a onetime thing or the basis for a lasting relationship. He hoped for the latter. Jeliyah was his. Her near death had solidified that notion for him.

He planned to keep her, no matter what.

CHAPTER

TWELVE

Jeliyah dribbled water through her fingers so she could watch it fall. The large tub full of water scented with lavender and chamomile soothed her nerves. She needed that after the week she'd had. Half of it didn't seem real, and yet her new life's direction was proof that it had happened.

A knock at the bathroom door drew her attention.

Teaghan asked through the door, "You coming out, or am I coming in?"

She looked down at the water, contemplating his question. They needed to talk. That wouldn't happen if she was naked. She stood. "I'm coming out."

After wrapping herself in a fluffy robe, she exited the bathroom.

Teaghan sat on the bed with his bare back to her. His hair was loose of the cornrows and wet. The mid-back-length red mass dripped into the towel he had wrapped around his waist.

"I used the shower in the other room." Teaghan glanced back at her.

"Oh." Nervous energy made her shy.

She didn't want to do this, and yet she knew she couldn't avoid it. They hadn't spoken on the trip back, and both had slept as soon as they reached the bedroom. The silence persisting after they awoke made Jeliyah retreat to the bathroom to get clean and think of a way to break the ice.

"Redo it."

"What?"

He jabbed a finger at his head. "My hair. Re-braid it."

Jeliyah snapped, "Just because I'm Black doesn't mean I automatically know how to braid hair."

"And I didn't say anything about your color. Stop acting indignant when we both know you can do it." He stood. "Now, where do you want me?"

She couldn't argue with him because he was right. Yet another fact about her that he'd pulled from her mind without her permission. She gestured to one of the easy chairs near the roaring fireplace. "On the floor."

Teaghan waited for her to gather the hair supplies and sit on the chair before he sat on the floor between her parted legs. He looped his arms over her knees, which forced her robe open and exposed her pussy. She pulled the halves of the robe together in a futile effort to cover herself. She should have dressed before coming out here.

It irked her that Teaghan didn't seem to care about her unease. He was relaxed and waiting for her to start. This position was probably one he'd been in tons of times with hundreds of other women. Jeliyah wondered how many times hair braiding had led to sex for him.

"None," he said softly. "I learned to braid my own hair. I've been doing it ever since."

"Really?" She touched his head, remembering the neat rows. "You did a great job."

"Decades of practice. And that was me being lazy. I was in a hurry when I did the last 'do. Give me something better."

She nodded, then picked up the brush and started pulling it

through his hair. She decided a spaced basket weave of braids would look good. Sectioning off a hunk of hair with the rattail comb, she started plaiting. As she became more comfortable with motion, she moved faster until she was using her vampire speed.

She'd finished half his head in a matter of minutes before she asked, "Why did you apologize?"

Teaghan grunted a questioning noise.

"In the forest, after… You apologized. Why?"

"That. Yeah." He tapped his palms against her legs. "I fucked up your life, so I apologized."

"You didn't."

"How do you figure? You're a vampire now because of me and the shit I got you into."

"I'm free of the campus now because of you. Niccolo was right. The only way to be free of them is death. Recognize started the bond, but it probably wouldn't have been enough. I would have spent the rest of my life dreading the day when I finally had to return." She smiled at the back of his head. "You changed that for me. There's no going back, no more threat. I feel like I have a life, now that I'm dead."

"You're not dead. You're just not mortal any longer."

She nodded.

Silence fell between them once more, and she continued her task. She was putting the last elastic band in place less than five minutes later when the image of an axe swinging in front of her eyes made her jerk back with a startled cry.

The axe stopped.

"Relax," Teaghan said in a monotone. "It's a memory. My memory."

"Teaghan?"

"Just watch."

She nodded and tried to relax once more as the axe resumed a swing that ended buried in Teaghan's chest. He stared at the axe, reaching for it with shaking hands. He wanted to pull it free, but the pain made it impossible. His blood-streaked gaze traveled to the face of the man who'd swung the axe—Gutun, his older brother.

Jeliyah asked in a breathy voice, "Your own brother? Why?"

Teaghan of the present and Gutun in the memory said in unison, "You're weak, little brother. I'll not have you bring ruin to our clan with talks of marriage and compromise because you've no stomach for battle. Die like the coward you are."

It took her a moment to digest the words before she realized what was wrong with them. "But you said you loved to kill. That you became a vampire on the battlefield."

"I did. My sire pulled the axe from my chest and raised me from mortal death to be a vampire. Bred from a warrior clan, I was trained and honed to fight, yet I yearned for peace. All in my family saw it as weakness except my father, who felt that peace served his clan better than battles with uncertain outcomes and great losses to the next generation.

"My father was clan chief, and I a favored son. To keep me from swaying his thinking any more than I had, my brother killed me during a skirmish with a rival clan. He then blamed the clan for my death and used that to rally my father into fighting on."

Teaghan rubbed her leg with an absentminded gesture. "The girl I was to marry to solidify the peace was made my brother's whore when he captured her. He abused her because she had belonged to me. Her family retaliated to get her back. When the dust settled, both clans were half what they were and easy pickings for a third clan who swooped in and massacred them both."

Jeliyah didn't know what to do, so she hugged his shoulders. Teaghan was sharing his life with her. As he spoke, his memories flitted through her mind, vivid as though she watched a movie. He'd forgotten nothing in all this time.

Teaghan said, "I watched it all. Forbidden by my sire from interfering, but forced to bear witness. In the span of seven years, I saw my family fall into ruin before the last of my blood was led from our ancestral land with a chain around his neck. I could only shake my head at the stupidity before turning my back on them. I haven't set foot on that land since."

"Why did he make you watch?"

"To harden my heart. My sire needed warriors to build his empire. He had dreams of being a head of his own family and finished the training my family started, gave me a taste for killing I'd never had before." He snorted a derisive laugh. "Then the damn fool went and got himself killed. His little army didn't match his ambition. I barely escaped with my life. I've been freelance ever since."

"Did you love her?"

Images of the girl Teaghan had tried to marry while he'd been human entered Jeliyah's mind. Her laughter echoed through all of Teaghan's memories. It was the one definite thing he remembered about her while her face was a blur. It wasn't lost on Jeliyah that he could recall every gory detail of his clan's massacre, but not the face of the woman he'd wanted to marry.

He said, "I might have. I remember I found her pretty enough and wanted to fuck her." He shrugged.

The nonchalant answer hurt her heart more than she cared to admit. She asked in a soft, uncertain voice, "Do you love me?"

Teaghan jerked around and met her gaze with a hard one. "Do you want me to love you, Jeliyah?" He moved to his knees, framed her head with his hands, and held her as he put his face close to hers. "See me, necromancer. See all of me and then tell me if you want the love of a man like me."

Images of blood, destruction, and glee at having caused it entered her mind. A strangled cry of pain and fear escaped Jeliyah's throat. Teaghan's past rushed through her mind like a video on fast-forward. Killing and fucking. Fucking and killing. Killing while fucking.

Teaghan's life had followed the same pattern for the last three hundred years. If there was a war, he'd been in the middle of it, not caring for which side he fought so long as he got to kill. At the time of the vampire outing, he'd adopted his new persona. It hadn't been gangsta back then. It had started out as soul and graduated into gangsta as time passed and trends changed.

No matter how he'd looked on the outside, Teaghan remained a killer within. All else he did was a momentary distraction between bloodshed. If it didn't make him money, get him laid, or lead to him killing something, he didn't care about it.

Tears streamed down Jeliyah's cheeks through Teaghan's fingers. He didn't let her go when she tried to pull away, to block the images. He'd opened the floodgates, drowning her in his mind, letting her have all of what she'd thought she wanted, all at once.

Now she knew why he'd blocked his thoughts from her, only letting her see what he allowed. Everything else was too gruesome for idle curiosity. Nothing could have prepared her for the life and times of a man who lived to see things die.

The rapid parade of macabre stopped with the sound of a door opening.

Jeliyah recognized the inside of Hirsch's office. Through Teaghan's memories, she smelled her cocoa-butter hair products mixed with her cucumber-and-aloe body wash. The scent had stirred his arousal and distracted him from his anger at being pulled off a rogue hunt.

Seeing her for the first time, Teaghan could have sworn his heartbeat sped up. He wanted her. More than any woman before, he wanted Jeliyah. Every word she spoke demanded his attention. Every movement caught his eye. He'd gone to the rogue hunt as a distraction from her.

Going back to the motel after their introduction instead of the hunt would have led to sex, with or without an invitation. He'd found ways around the invitation before. Necromancer or not, Jeliyah wouldn't have been an exception to his seduction.

Their first kiss, when she'd taken his blood, had shoved all reality from his mind except her. If Jeliyah had said the word, he would have forgotten Dumas, ignored the threat of death, and fucked her then and there. Dumas could have killed Teaghan and he would have died a happy man so long as it was after he got to taste Jeliyah.

Her tears flowed harder, but a shaky smile curved her lips as Teaghan revealed himself. She saw herself through his eyes. Eyes that appeared pained at having laid himself so bare.

She closed the distance between them, placing her lips against his. Teaghan buried his hand in her hair as he made the kiss deeper, harder. He bruised her lips, and she took the pain because it reflected his love.

Jeliyah had had to use Recognize and Resonate before she admitted to her feelings, but Teaghan had come to terms with his from the start.

{Say you want me, damn it. Say it. And if you don't want me, I'm not giving you up.} Teaghan indulged images of tying her to the bed for his pleasure as a means of keeping her with him.

{Sounds fun. We can do that later. You promised to spank me first though.}

He startled and pulled back, staring at Jeliyah in surprise. After a moment, he chuckled and shook his head. "Always the quiet ones into the freaky shit."

She laid a kiss on his nose. "You're the one into the freaky shit. All the threats of spankings and tying me up are coming from you. I'm just letting you know I'm game when you are."

"That's it." Teaghan shoved her so she fell back against the chair before he spread her thighs wide and jammed his face against her pussy. He made loud slurping noises as he licked her slit and sucked her clit.

Jeliyah arched her back, jutting her hips up and hooking her legs around his shoulders to hold him close. "Right there! Oh yes, Teaghan! Yes, please!"

He gripped her ass and held her steady for his deep kiss, pushing his tongue into her twitching pussy. He delved deep, licking and wriggling. The more she squirmed against his hold, the faster he moved.

This wasn't like the time in the forest. Jeliyah had an idea what to expect now. The sensations were still intense and overwhelmed her to a degree she couldn't comprehend, but she craved the onslaught.

She screamed her release so loud the windows shook against their frames. She remained tensed and trapped in the orgasm until Teaghan removed his mouth. The second his hot lips no longer touched her, she wanted them back.

"Got something better for you," Teaghan said as he stood.

With her ankles resting on his shoulders, Teaghan spread her labia with one hand while guiding his erection forward with the other. He completed the contact with a single thrust forward.

Savoring the connection took a backseat as Teaghan moved. He surged forward, circled his hips so his hard length stirred her inside, and then pulled back only to do it all again. Jeliyah moved with him, squeezing her inner muscles each time he retreated.

{That's right, sweetness. Suck that dick.}

She grinned at him, eager to give as good as he was giving. This was more than pleasure for them. It was a solidifying of their new relationship. She knew Teaghan now, truly knew him. He'd opened his mind and his heart to her and shown her that Recognize hadn't been a mistake.

Every thrust hammered that fact home, and Jeliyah would never be able to deny or question it again.

Teaghan's satisfied growling rumbled through his body to hers until she was doing it, too. Hers turned to passionate keens as he spread her legs so he could play her clit.

He passed his fingers over the sensitive nub in a melody of her. A pinch got a whimper. A flick made her yip. She panted when he rolled her clit between two fingers and moaned when he rubbed.

"Sing my tune, necromancer." He mixed his movements like

mixing music at the club, with the slap of his skin against hers provided the bass.

As much as Jeliyah wanted the song to last, Teaghan felt too delicious for his own good. She was coming again. No amount of holding it back would stop the momentum from building. She held her arms open instead, wanting to feel more of him than his pounding of his length inside her.

Teaghan leaned forward into her embrace. She wound her arms around his shoulders and tangled her fingers in his braids. His lips met hers as she climaxed.

{I love you.} Jeliyah cried the words from her mind to his because she couldn't speak them, didn't want to let him go to use her voice.

{Then don't let go, Jeliyah. I'm all yours.} Teaghan surged forward, burying his dick as deep as it would go, and spilled himself with his release. He grinned against her lips as his tongue dueled with hers.

A knock at the door distracted them from a second round.

Teaghan backed out of Jeliyah and helped her get situated, closing her robe and pulling her to an upright position with her legs together before he bid the knocker enter.

Mekhail opened the door and stood in the threshold, wearing a knowing grin. "Niccolo has called you, sire, miss. He has a hunt for you."

Teaghan sucked his teeth in disgust. "Damn, man. He couldn't give us a night?"

"Seems not, sire. Do you want me to recommend to him that he choose another?"

Jeliyah said over Teaghan's would-be reply, "No, we'll be there shortly. Thanks, Mekhail."

"You're welcome, miss." He nodded to them and pulled the door closed as he left.

To Teaghan, she said, "You like killing things."

"I like fucking you more. I had plans to go all night." He rolled his eyes. "Whatever. Let's get this done."

Jeliyah grinned at his back. Teaghan was cute when he pouted. She wanted him to keep loving her, but a small break would make the return that much hotter.

She rushed through dressing, but Teaghan finished before her. He waited by the bedroom door, his grumpy attitude still in place. He even pulled away with an annoyed grunt when she tried to give him a kiss.

That made her laugh. She decided to let him have his little temper tantrum.

"I'm not having a temper tantrum."

"Uh-huh." She walked out of the room in front of him. With a mischievous smile she said a singsong, "Teaghan."

"What?" he snapped.

She flipped up the back of her knee-length skirt and bent forward with her ass out, revealing the open-zippered crotch of her full-body catsuit. She wiggled her hips while pressing her thighs together so her pussy lips puckered at him. A little down-under kiss blowing.

Teaghan stared for a moment before shaking his head hard, as though trying to wake himself from a stupor. The front of his loose pants tented. "Damn, you know how to put a man in a good mood quick."

She lowered her skirt and straightened with a smile. "Thought you might like that."

He rushed her, crowding her against the wall. Before he could kiss her, she placed a hand over his mouth. A little nudge got him to back up one step.

She said in a coy voice, "We have a hunt. When it's over, then you can have what I showed you, any way and every way you want." She moved her hand and laid a kiss on his nose. "If you behave. Deal?"

Niccolo had only invited them into his home and employ a few days ago. It wouldn't do to have Teaghan's bad attitude ruin that. If the promise of sex made him act right, she was happy to give it.

"Deal," Teaghan rasped.

She nodded and started walking again, and Teaghan fell into step beside her. She stumbled when his hand found its way between her legs and he swept one finger back and forth over her wet slit.

As much as she wanted to indulge the sweet sensations his touch invoked, they had a meeting to attend. He hooked two fingers in her slick channel, and Jeliyah had to stop. They hadn't had nearly enough sex for her to be acclimated to the rush of arousal and overpowering need that resulted from such a simple touch. She shivered as he moved his fingers in and out of her.

Teaghan leaned close and whispered, "If you manage not to make a sound during the meeting with Niccolo—" he yanked his hand upward, pulling a mewl of need from her "—I'll finish this in the car. Deal?"

She bit her lip and nodded. Somehow, her little ploy had been turned against her.

"You're too young to go up against me, necromancer. Lucky for you, this game has no losers." He urged her forward with his fingers still inside her pussy to start her walking again.

They entered Niccolo's study, and Jeliyah tried to act cool. Nothing to see here. Everything was completely normal. Except Niccolo's knowing smile showed he knew what was happening.

Teaghan said, "I thought you said you had enough necro-vamps that you didn't need an enforcer, Niccolo."

Niccolo chuckled. "Necro-vamps. Such a quaint term. I might have to use it. And while I have quite a few, I know better than to let a man like you get bored, Teaghan."

"I'm not."

"Not now, you aren't. But your—" he swept his gaze over Jeliyah "—little entertainments won't feed the killer in you for long."

"True that. So what do you got?"

"A rogue who doesn't know any better. It should be a quick and easy hunt for you."

"Good. I had plans for this evening."

"So I'm noticing." He laughed a little as his gaze trailed down to Jeliyah's skirt.

The front appeared normal and didn't betray Teaghan's displacement of the back or the rhythmic in-and-out movement of his fingers as he stuffed her pussy from behind. His movements made no noise, which surprised her considering how wet she was. It took all of Jeliyah's concentration to hold back her sounds of pleasure while Niccolo outlined the coming hunt.

She heard none of what he said, and the man's grin grew more and more amused as the meeting wore on. In fact, she swore he and Teaghan started small talk to prolong her torture.

{I can fuck you here and now, if you want. Give Niccolo a show. I'm sure he wouldn't mind.} Teaghan moved faster, pumping his fingers so her juices started churning loud enough that everyone in the room had to hear them. {You game, necromancer?}

Jeliyah found herself weighing her options instead of denying the proposal outright. She didn't used to be the exhibitionist type. A few days with Teaghan, and she was baring her breasts for strangers as well as letting him finger-fuck her while in a meeting about a rogue hunt. What had happened to her?

{Told you. You's a freak. You just needed the right man to bring it out of you.} Teaghan removed his fingers and patted her ass before smoothing down her skirt. To Niccolo he said, "We'll get it done."

Niccolo tented his fingers. "I'm sure you will. Have fun."

Teaghan grinned. "I plan to."

"I meant with the hunt, Teaghan."

"I'll have fun doing that too." Teaghan slipped his arm around Jeliyah's waist and helped her walk out of the office.

Every step vibrated pleasure through her. She couldn't do the hunt keyed up like this. All her senses were tuned to Teaghan. The rogue could walk up to her and spit in her face, and she probably wouldn't see him.

The car ride wasn't much better. The vibrations from the engine and the rumbling road beneath the tires further excited her sensitive pussy. Pressing her thighs together didn't alleviate the sensation.

As Teaghan drove down the highway, her gaze strayed to the bulge he'd had since she flashed him earlier. How could he act as if everything was normal when he was sporting wood hard enough that his dick was pointing up at the stars? How desperate was she that she considered hopping on it while he was driving?

First, there wasn't room. Second, she doubted Teaghan could keep driving with her bouncing on his lap.

"So I'll pull over." He cut across three lanes of traffic—several angry drivers shouted curses and leaned on their horns—to the shoulder and slammed the car in park. After unzipping his pants, he patted his thighs.

Jeliyah didn't hesitate. It was tight, even after Teaghan moved the seat back, but Jeliyah managed to fit on his lap with his dick buried deep in her pussy. They couldn't open the door without the chance of a passing car hitting it, so she draped her leg over it instead.

"Let's do this." Teaghan bucked, which bounced Jeliyah's ass off the car horn. A few of the passing cars honked back.

She laughed, though her amusement didn't last long as the pleasure of the moment overtook her. She grabbed the top of the windshield and used it to help her snake her torso.

A move that got Teaghan licking his lips and nodding. "That's the way, sweetness. You know what I like."

"What we both like."

He leaned forward, grabbed the zipper tag at her collar with his teeth, and pulled it down. The catsuit split open, revealing her breasts to Teaghan's hungry gaze. He licked both her nipples in rapid succession. His vampiric speed made it seem as though he had two mouths that pleasured her simultaneously.

She let her head fall back with her eyes closed and enjoyed the moment. The future flashed before her—fucking at ninety miles per hour described it best. They would fight. They would love. They would drive each other insane with pleasure. But most of all, they would be together.

About the Author

Zenobia Renquist is the alter ego of D. Reneé Bagby. Friends call her Renee. An Air Force brat turned Air Force (retired) wife, she has lived in multiple countries and states before settling in Maryland. She's an avid world builder who loves torturing her characters on the way to happily ever after or happily for the moment. When not concocting new ways to give her characters a hard time, she enjoys crocheting, reading isekai and danmei, watching anime, and bingeing C-dramas and K-dramas in the historical and fantasy genres.

- **Pronouns:** She / Her / Mrs.
- **Relationship:** Married (cis / het)
- **Children:** None (2 cats)
- **Zodiac:** Sheep / Capricorn
- **Alignment:** Chaotic Good
- **Writer Type:** Pantser / Organic

https://zenobiarenquist.com/

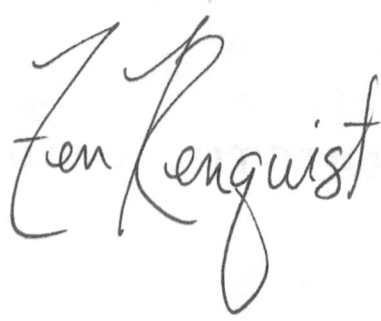

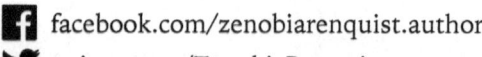

facebook.com/zenobiarenquist.author
twitter.com/ZenobiaRenquist
instagram.com/author_zenobiarenquist
bookbub.com/authors/zenobia-renquist
goodreads.com/zenobiarenquist